There Are Little Kingdoms

There Are Little Kingdoms

Stories

Kevin Barry

The Stinging Fly

A·Stinging Fly Press Book

There Are Little Kingdoms is first published simultaneously in paperback
and in a clothbound edition in March 2007.

The Stinging Fly Press
PO Box 6016
Dublin 8
www.stingingfly.org

Set in Palatino
Printed by Betaprint, Dublin

ISBN 978-0-9550152-6-7 (paperback)
978-0-9550152-5-0 (clothbound)

Earlier versions of some of these stories appeared in *The Adirondack Review*,
The Dublin Review, *The Stinging Fly*, *Phoenix Best Irish Stories 2001* (ed: David Marcus) and
These Are Our Lives (ed: Declan Meade). 'See The Tree, How Big It's Grown'
was shortlisted for the Davy Byrnes Irish Writing Award in 2004.

The Stinging Fly Press gratefully acknowledges the financial support of
The Arts Council/An Chomhairle Ealaíon in the publication of this title.

for Maura Meade

Contents

Atlantic City

A July evening, after a tar-melter of a day, and Broad Street was quiet and muffled with summer, the entire town was dozy with summer, and even as the summer peaked so it began to fade. Dogs didn't know what had hit them. They walked around the place with their tongues hanging out and their eyes rolling and they lapped forlornly at the drains. The old were anxious, too: they twitched the curtains to look to the hills, and flapped themselves with copies of the *RTE Guide* to make a parlour breeze. Later, after dark, the bars would be giddy with lager drinkers, but it was early yet, and Broad Street was bare and peaceful in the blue evening.

The youth of Broad Street and its surrounds had convened in a breeze-block arcade tacked onto Moloney's Garage. This had been one of Moloney's sharper moves. He'd taken an old shed that he'd used for a store room, it was maybe forty foot long and half as wide, and he'd installed there a pool table, three video games, a wall-mounted jukebox and a pinball machine. To add a note of local pride, he'd painted the walls in the county colours. It wasn't much of an arcade, with just the clack and nervous roll of the pool balls, and the insipid bleats of Donkey Kong and Defender. There was high anxious talk about girls and handjobs and who had cigarettes, and there was talk about cars and motorbikes. It wasn't much at all but it was the only show in town and this evening, a dozen habituees had gathered there, all boys, from pre-pubescents through to late teens, and there was desperation to make this a different kind of night, a night to sustain them through the long winter. But so far it was the same old routine, with Donkey Kong and Defender, and winner-stays-on at the pool table, and James was always the winner, and he always stayed on. The pinball machine lit up and crackled to salute a good score. Its theme was the criminal scene of Atlantic City, and the illustration showed a black detective, with a heavy moustache, patrolling in a red sports car, and whenever the day's hi-score was achieved, the detective's eyes lit up and he spoke out, in a deep-voiced, downtown drawl.

He said: 'Atlantic City. Feel The Force!'

This was James's cue to leave the pool table and approach the pinball machine. At nineteen, he was the oldest of the habituees, and certainly the biggest. Not fat so much as massive, the width of a small van across the shoulders, and he moved noiselessly, as though on castors, and the flesh swung and rolled with him, there was no little grace to it, and he considered the breathless, blushing youngster who'd achieved a new hi-score on Atlantic City, and he considered the score, and he said:

'Handy. Handy alright.'

With a long-suffering sigh he reached deep into the pocket of his jeans and took out the necessary coin and inserted it in the slot. The silver balls slapped free and he pulled the spring-release to send the first of them on its way, and it bounced and pinged and rebounded around the nooks and contours of the game, around the boardwalks and the neon boulevards, and wordlessly, the habituees of the arcade swivelled their attention from the pool to the pinball, for the magic had shifted to a new discipline, and cigarette smoke hung blue in the air, and it twisted as they turned. It was a matter of pride to James that he wouldn't let even one of the silver balls drop between the flippers to the dead-ball zone, and he worked the flippers with quick rhythmic slaps from his fingers and palms—an expert—and his score rolled onwards and upwards. The habituees were hypnotised by the ratcheting numbers, and James knew precisely when he'd made the day's hi-score and he drawled it deep, in time with the black detective:

'Atlantic City. Feel The Force!'

Then, with the silver ball still pinging and rebounding, and the score climbing still higher, his routine was to become Stevie Wonder. He closed his eyes and clamped on a delirious smile and rocked his head wildly from side to side, and he sang:

'Happy Birthday… Happy Birthday to ya… Happpy Biiiiirthday…'

And the arcade rumbled with the usual low laughter, and as James sang the blind star's signature tune and rocked his head on his huge shoulders, beaming blindly to the ceiling, he let the flippers miss the first of the silver balls, and he released the second and let that drop too, and then the third, and all the while he maintained the delirium of a blind ecstatic. Then he returned to the pool table, took up his cue, and said:

'Right so. Where am I here?'

'You're on the reds, Jamesie.'

Beyond the open doors of the arcade, Broad Street revelled in the unexpected langour of evening heat. Broad Street didn't know itself. The evening was moving to its close, quicker now as the summer aged, but there was heat in it still. There was scant traffic. The hills above the town darkened with the shadows of approaching night. Moloney sat in his kiosk, on the forecourt of the garage, by the pumps, and he cursed the championship reports in the weekly paper. The lying bastards hadn't seen the same match he'd seen. They were making excuses for the county side. He hadn't seen a county side as weak in years. There were fellas with weight on them. It was a disgrace. There were fellas on the county side who'd spent the winter drinking. Where, Moloney asked the walls of his kiosk, oh where was the dedication? There were no answers, and certainly none outside on Broad Street.

James chalked his cue. He performed this action with priestly nuance, a sense of ritual. He allowed a particular amount of chalk onto the tip's head, blew off the excess dust, and then, with an air of dainty finesse, surprising in a young man the width of a van, he chalked the curved sides of the tip too. A small fat pink tongue emerged from between his lips as he performed the task. It was a sign of concentration, for it was a knacky business to get it right. He wanted no moisture whatsoever in the vicinity of the cue's tip. Not on a night so clammy as this, when the arcade was fuggy with the sweat and vapours of teenagers in summer.

'So listen, Carmody,' he said. 'Are you looking at me with a straight face on you and telling me she's not ridin'?'

'All I'm saying is I don't think our friend has been next nor near. Our friend hasn't been within a million miles.'

James closed his eyes, briefly, and nodded his head, slowly. This was sombre acknowledgement of information received. His manner, as he leaned in over the pool table, was proper and studious. The great mass of his belly he arranged carefully, and he peeked beneath his chin to ensure that it was not interfering with play and thus causing a foul—if it was, he'd be the first to call it—and he formed a careful bridge for the cue between thumb and forefinger of the left hand, and he sized up a long red for the bottom left corner.

'I'm not saying for a minute she'd be an auld slut,' he said. 'I'm not saying that at all. All I'm saying is she'd be gamey. All I'm sayin' is if you could get her going at all then she'd really go for you. Do you know what I mean, Carm? She'd be like...'

His gaze drifted out to Broad Street, as he sought the precise image.

'She'd be like a little motorbike.'

The low murmur of laughter rippled again around the table's edges. Another kid was having a go at Atlantic City, there was an amount of interest in Defender, somewhat less in Donkey Kong, but there was no contesting the focus of attention. Outside, at a little past nine, the evening had gone into tawn, was in its dream-time, with the sky velvet, with the air still warm, with the shadows taking on the precise tone of the sky's glow. As he prepared to let the cue slide, James tapped the faded baize three times with the middle finger of his bridge hand, a sportsman's tic, and with his right arm working from the elbow as a smooth piston, he made the shot. He sent the white down the table onto the red and its kiss sent the red slowly for the bottom left, and the left-hand side he had applied to the cue ball, an indescribable delicacy, caused it to drag and spin back towards the centre of the table, where it would be ideally in

place for the next red he had in mind. The object red still rolled, slowly, and then it dropped into the bottom left pocket, and the cue ball's
positioning was perfect, and his opponent, Carmody, tapped the butt
of his cue three times on the concrete floor in stony-faced regard. And
the usual hymn, the usual evensong, was sung:

'Shot, James.'

'Shot, Jamesie.'

'Shot.'

'Shot, boy.'

The hymn was ignored, was disdained. He leaned for a tap-in red
to the middle right, its ease a result of his positional play, and he
made it without fuss. A lesser player would be inclined to ram in the
easier pots with showy force and venom, but always James played
the game quietly, he would roll his reds gently home rather than slam
them, he would apply no more force than was needed, and for this
reason it was exquisite to watch him play, and the arcade was hushed
in the presence of his talent.

Just then, the air changed: a small troop of girls arrived in, a bat-
talion of three. They had vinegar in them and they roved their dangerous eyes around the habitutees and they were a carnival of cheap
perfume on young skin and whatever summer was they'd trapped
its essence and fizzed with it. The habituees developed deeper
slouches, and their heads went shyly down, and they moved back
into the shadows if they could, but their eyes were uncontrollable
and darted up insanely for an eyeful of suntanned girl and they
couldn't but wince from the delirious pain of it. All the boys became
awkward like this, and thick-tongued, all except James. He laid the
cue across the table, rubbed his meaty hands together, straightened
his shoulders, closed his eyes, shook his head in wonderment and he
said:

'Ladies? I'll say one thing now for nothing. I've seen ye lookin'
well in yere time but never as well as ye're lookin' tonight.'

It was the girls' turn to be shy. His hungry gaze asked severe
questions of their confidence and inside they seethed at being
reduced to these giggles, this nudging. They went and staked out the
ground around the wall-mounted jukebox, it was their acknowl-

edged terrain, and they hummed and hawed over the selections and James strode across the floor, searched for another coin in the pocket of his big jeans as he moved, and with a polite gesture of the hand moved the girls back a little from the jukebox and put the coin in the slot and selected the song that was currently at the top of the charts. He took the cue from the table to use as a microphone and he launched powerfully into song as 'Baby Jane' by Rod Stewart struck up on the tinny speakers, and he planted his feet wide on the floor, rock star fashion, and he had all the required shimmies of hip and flicks of hair, and laughter took hold of the arcade, again, and everybody was relaxed and easy again.

A farm truck pulled up on the forecourt outside, and dispensed a farmer, and Moloney shrugged out of his kiosk and nodded curtly, and received a curt nod in payment, and Moloney crossed his arms and leaned back against the pumps.

'That was some messin' below in Clancy Park on Sunday,' said Moloney.

'Shocking,' said the farmer.

'There're fellas should be shot,' said Moloney.

'Don't be talking to me,' agreed the farmer.

'You could put stones in jerseys and you'd get more out of them.'

'You nearly could.'

'But listen to me, did you have any joy with them creatures above?'

The farmer looked to the velvet sky, and he considered the vagaries of life, chance, and sheep management.

'There's no getting them down off that blasted hill,' he said. 'I'm going to have to come up with a new tactic.'

And Broad Street was on fire. The last of the evening gave out in a show of dying golds and reds. The street lamps came on. The blue flicker of television screens could be seen behind terrace windows. The summer night announced itself, with its own starlit energies. It brought temptation, yearning and ache, because these are the summer things.

James slotted a straight red into the top left pocket, and he applied top spin to the cue ball so that it rolled onto the top cushion and allowed him to line up the last of the reds. This would be tricky, because great precision was required when the cushions came into play, and he lit a cigarette to consider it. Carmody was his opponent, again, and he was all but beaten anyway, Carmody was beaten in the mind even before they began to play, but all the same James liked to win stylishly and well, he liked to make little gasps escape the habituees when he achieved the unlikely shots. He paused now to draw attention to the table before he attempted the difficult red.

'You're putting it up to me tonight, Carm,' he said. 'I don't know what's after getting into you but you've moved on to a new level of expertise altogether. Are you practicing on the sly?'

The habituees quietened, and moved in closer, because they could sense a put-down in the making. James had gone into the familiar pose, with the head held at a slight incline, and he regarded Carmody down his nose, and there was a thin set to the mouth, and he expelled air from the nostrils with a powerful snort, and he said:

'You're practicing on the sly in the barn, aren't you? You're like…'

He put the cue down and danced a two-step.

'You're like an auld farmer hitting off to a matchmaking festival. He's had the first bath of the year. He has the hair slicked back with strong tea. He's dragged a comb through his teeth…'

The titters and giggles built nervously, as the habituees waited to see where James would take it.

'…and he's set the hens on automatic. He's worried about the dancing, of course he is, the man has titanium hips, so he's clearin' back the floor of the barn, of an evening, when the working day is done, and he's trying out a shtep.'

And he did a high-kick step in the air, and the laughter rumbled, and built.

'And he's saying what I need for myself now is… a nice good lit-tle nurse. Do you know the way? A nice little nurse from an ear, nose and throat ward. He's always maintained a bit of a grá for nurses, because they'd be kind to you, wouldn't they, of a cold winter's night, with the big thighs wrapped around your throat?'

The girls gasped and tssked. The habituees shook their heads, embarrassed with mirth. They never knew where to look when

James roamed abroad on a course.

'It's the way I see it, Carm. You're practicing on the sly in the barn, like the auld farmer, by the light of a lonesome moooo-oooon!'

And as he crooned the word, cowboy-style, he leaned in to attend to his shot: full attention had now been secured for the pool table. He made his bridge, tapped the baize three times with his middle finger, rolled the white along the cushion, it kissed the red, and gave it momentum to move at a slow even pace, and the red yawned for a moment on the lip of the pocket, as though he hadn't given it enough, but of course he had, and it dropped.

'Shot, James!'

'Shot, Jamesie.'

'Shot boy.'

'You're a fucking lunatic, James,' said Carmody, and tapped the butt of his cue three times on the concrete floor.

'Sure I know that.'

Moloney put the petrol takings into a tin box, turned off the transistor and locked up the kiosk. He crossed the forecourt, carrying the tin box reverently, and he cursed at the weather. Ten o'clock at night and you were walking around the place in soup. He put his head around the door of the arcade.

'Ye've an hour till I close it up.'

'Not a bother,' said James.

'And keep it down a bit, for Jesus' sake.'

'Absolutely,' said James.

'An hour,' said Moloney. 'D'ye hear me?'

James laid the cue on the table, goose-stepped across the floor, threw his right arm into salute and cried out:

'Selbstverständlich, mein Kommandant!'

'And you watch yourself!'

Moloney tried and failed to keep the smile from his face, and he left them to it. This was the signal that the night was truly rolling, and for the more dangerous talk to begin. The younger of the habituees, earlier indulged, would now be pushed to the peripheries. The older ones would draw up schemes of devilment for the small hours. The girls became nervous.

'Atlantic City. Feel The Force!'

'Ah for the love and honour of God,' said James, who had been lining up the black to continue his evening-long winning streak. He crossed the floor to the pinball, considered the new hi-score, patted his young usurper on the head and said:

'Knacky. Knacky alright. As a matter of fact, you've put it beyond my reach. Let it be known that from this moment forward, the young fella here is the king of the pinball. Give the boy a banana.'

Walking back to the pool table, James suddenly stopped, gasped, and collapsed onto his knees. He clutched at his chest. His face was frozen in a terrible grin, and it became a grimace, and he gasped out the last words...

'I... leave... every... thing... to... to... to Jamesie!'

The arcade throbbed with laughter. This was one of the most famed routines. It was James's impression of the heart attack that had killed his father on the kitchen floor.

Though the girls had become shyer, shyness can fold in on itself and be transformed on a summer night: when there is possibility in the air, shyness can say what the hell and trade itself for a brazenness. They fed coins to the jukebox and summoned a couple of slow numbers.

James saw to the black, and allowed his next opponent to step forward and rack for a new game, and he moved his great rolling flesh to the jukebox, and he said:

'Ladies? Ye'll have me red in the face now for the want of it. Do ye hear what I'm saying? Is there no such as thing as a bit of mercy? Ye know full well what I'm like when I hear that one. I hear Bonnie Tyler and I go to pieces.'

The younger of the habituees began to drift off, in ones and twos, and those who left early would be furious the next morning, when they learned that they'd missed the great drama of the night. A little before eleven, the squad car rolled into the forecourt of Moloney's, and Garda Ryan got out, with a face on him like turned milk. He stood on the forecourt and regarded the arcade, and everybody crowded to the door, and he addressed them.

'There was a windscreen of a car put in below in the square last night,' he said. 'Is that news for ye?'

James moved to the front of the habituees, crossed his arms sombrely, and stroked his chin with his forefinger.

'At what time precisely, Garda Ryan,' he said, 'was the mechanically propelled vehicle interfered with?'

'Watch yourself.'

'Have you no note made of it, guard?'

'I won't warn you again. Believe me! I don't care who your family is. There was a windscreen put in. That's a hundred pound damage. There's been other incidents. There's been nothing but trouble since this place was let open late. I'm marking yere cards for ye now, all of ye. I've eyes in my head and they are wide open. I'm not going to let this messing go on a night longer. Not a single night, d'ye hear it? I'm watching ye.'

Garda Ryan, in shirt sleeves, stepped back into the squad car, and with a flinty gaze he looked over the small group from his rolled-down window, and the more nervous of the habituees stepped back into the gloom, but it could not be left at this, and it wouldn't be, and one of them stepped out onto the forecourt, and everybody held their breath, because it was James. He planted his feet wide, gunslinger style, and mimicked a pair of pistols with his fingers and thumbs, and he drew and aimed at the guard, and he said:

'Atlantic City. Feel The Force!'

There were still tears and peals of laughter when Moloney came back to lock up, and Moloney had a few drinks on him, and he was convinced that he himself was the cause of the merriment, and he became narky.

'Feck off home out of it!' he cried. 'I'm seriously thinking of closing this place altogether! I'm seriously thinking of calling a halt to the whole bastarin' operation!'

And they set off about the town. The last of the younger ones straggled home with regret, because July nights like this don't come around too often. The older ones caused what trouble they could, even though in a small town it was hard to work out constant variations on trouble, but they tried anyway. The summer night was warm and sweet about them, and repeated assaults were made upon the reputations of the girls. The summer would move on, and fade, there is always the terrible momentum of the year's turning. Exam results would come in. The older of the habituees would begin to make their moves. For one that would move to the city, another would stay in the town, some would take up the older trades, others would try out new paths, and one on a low September evening would swim out too far and drown, and it would be James. Laments and regrets were no use—these were just the quotas and insistences of Broad Street.

To The Hills

The way it is in this country, he said, someone sees you out walking a hill and you're a fucking eejit. Just because you're not in the pub or in front of the television watching crap. I will tell you one thing, Teresa, I would rather be walking the hills than listening to some of the fuckers around this place.

Teresa nodded, sighed, mewed.

It was a good old hike today, he said. You kept up well, the two of you. You found the North Faces did the job? Yes, well, what did I tell you? The North Face is an excellent boot. A good boot is something it's worth your while you spend a few quid on. There is no point codding yourself with cheap boots, Teresa. The Goretex is an outstanding material, we know that, anybody can tell you that. Reliable, I wouldn't be caught dead with anything else. You found the dried fruit a help? Good. It beats a Mars Bar, you know? With the dried fruit and the nuts, you see, it's a slow release of energy that you get, just what you need at the tail end of a grade five.

He had furious eyebrows perched up top of a dismal nose. He wore a helmet of sandy, wiry hair. He was the guts of six foot.

Well, Teresa, he said, this is Wicklow, this is March, what were you expecting exactly? This isn't the Canaries we're talking about. Anyway, you don't feel it with the fleece on you. From the way you were going on, the two of you, I thought you were well used to the hills. Hah? This is what I was led to believe, Teresa.

They had met at the hillwalking club in Dublin that winter. The club put leaflets in outdoorsy shops and sometimes a small ad in the paper. It met Tuesdays, year-round, at a well-lit suburban lounge bar: all welcome. It was mostly country people that showed up, and most of them were past the first flush. There would be two hours of shy talk over stretched drinks. Truth be told, Teresa and her friend, Marie, didn't have that much of an interest in hills but they had an interest in healthy men and Brian seemed steady, he had a good job in the labs on the campus, he didn't drink much, he was tall and slim. He wouldn't have figured himself for a catch but there you go.

I suppose you could say that I'm not great with people, Teresa, he said. I'll be straight with you now, women have always been difficult for me. It's a long time since I've been in a relationship of any kind. Which is a word I hate, by the way. The people at work we're having a drink or at lunchtime, what have you, it's my relationship this, my relationship that, blah blah blah. Another one is partner. Jesus! I hate that word. My partner this, my partner that, you can bring your partner, do you have a partner. Fuck off. Do you know what I'm saying to you? Fuck off! Partner, I don't know, it makes it sound like a badminton team.

They were naked together in bed, having not had sex.

I'll be perfectly straight with you, Teresa, why shouldn't I be? I haven't been with a woman for fourteen years. Drought isn't the word, Teresa. You'll be getting worried now, of course. You'll be thinking, what's with your man? But no, don't, listen, please. This is an absolutely amazing thing for me. It's like I don't know what's going on. Just to be lying here with you is unbelievable to me.

The plan had been: park in Wicklow town, walk the grade five to Tobar Pass, a bite to eat, a few drinks, stay the night at a B&B, walk back the next morning. They had booked three rooms. This had been complicated. Brian, obviously, was going to have a room to himself, but what were the girls going to do? If they shared a room, it meant they were marking each other for the night and what if something happened? They booked a room each. We might as well get a room each, they said, it's cheap. This was an unspoken declaration of combat. Two channels had thus opened up for Brian, though he was not at all sure that this was the case.

The B&B was run by a tiny woman who conversed in the small

hours of the night—every night—with an aunt dead twenty years. In the afternoon, when they got in, she put on her glasses and with a show of great ritual opened her bookings ledger. The bookings ledger gave her a tingling pleasure. It made her feel giddy and playful. When she opened that ledger she was like a cat with a ball of twine. She asked Marie and Teresa were they sure they didn't want to share a room, she had a fine double out back, it would be cheaper. The girls glared at her, they said no, thank you, no, we'll take the two. Brian flushed.

More money than sense! he said.

Crazy, said the tiny woman.

They went to their rooms, and each was glad of a short reprieve from company. These were single people, in their forties, each of them had lived alone for many years, and such a long morning of company was a trial. The rooms were pretty much identical. Each had a narrow bed with a lumpy mattress. Each had a wardrobe, a dresser, a tumbler, a cup and saucer, a kettle and teabags, sachets of Bewley's coffee that had lain there since the previous millennium. Each room had an en-suite bathroom that had been haphazardly plastered by the tiny woman's middle-aged nephew, a man who had savage dependency on drink, an addiction to cough bottles and a sullen, thyroidal glare. Marie's view was of a galvanised tin roof on a shed at the back of the house. She sat on the bed and stared at the green wallpaper. The wallpaper showed a jungle scene. It was green for calm. She could hear the shower running in Teresa's room next door.

Watch that bitch like a hawk, she said to herself.

If you were to ask me what it all goes back to, Teresa, said Brian, if you were to put me on the couch and say, well now, where does it all go back to? Tell me about your childhood, all that crap? Okay, fine, it's obviously all rooted down there.

Is that right? said Teresa

My father died suddenly, he said, when I was eight years of age. Yeah, I know, boo-hoo. But the way of it was the worst thing. It was shockingly sudden. A brain haemorrhage. We were on our holidays. We were at the beach! Yeah. One minute he's lying there in his togs, the next he's lying there dead. My brother and myself were playing in the dunes. Were you ever in Lahinch, Teresa? Unbelievable dunes and there we are, rolling around in the sand, pretending to be Buck Rogers on the moon, or what have you, and after a while we said we'll go back to Mam and Dad for the coke and crisps, you know, and when we go back, she's kneeling in the sand, bawling. She's going, John! Oh John! John! And my father is lying there on the towel with blood all over his neck. An amount of blood you would not believe.

Did you know that, he said, did you know, Teresa, that blood actually comes out the ears?

Go 'way? said Teresa.

Actually my most vivid memory isn't the beach but going back to Sligo the next day. My brother and myself, we were in shock I suppose but innocent—all we could talk about when they were putting him in the hearse in Lahinch is how long is a hearse going to take to get to Sligo? We worked it out. If a hearse goes five miles an hour and Sligo is a hundred miles away, that's twenty hours! It never dawned on us that the hearse would go at a normal speed until we got him home. We thought it was funeral pace all the way up through Clare and Galway. And this is the bit I remember vividly, isn't that strange? We're in the car, behind the hearse, with my mother up to the gills on tablets, she's cruising, and my uncle is driving and your man is driving the hearse in front of us through Clare and he must be doing seventy. And all I can remember is the coffin bouncing around in the back of the hearse and thinking, ah Jesus, that can't be right, like.

A few days later, myself and the brother are kicking a ball again, Teresa, we're children, we're Buck Rogers, and you get on with being a child, you do. But are you going to come out of it right?

After the morning's long walk, after they reached Tobar Pass, they went to a pub for lunch. Soup, toasties, cups of coffee. The pub was rich on hillwalkers and had lately been refitted. A brand new coffee machine gurgled like an excited aunt. The lunchtime rush was just about done, and the slow hours of the afternoon yawned and presented themselves with a certain belligerence. Those who go mad go mad first in the afternoons. There was the usual fall-out of day-time drinkers, glassy-eyed, with their hearty talk and guilty-seeming cheer. A silence had fallen in on the three hillwalkers, it had a knuckly and mannish grip.

Well, said Brian at last, I don't know about yourselves but I'm going to go out there and get the last of that daylight into me.

Don't tell me you're walking again? said Marie, who was out of puff still from the morning's exertion. She was a pretty but dour woman, with eyes full of dread and rain.

Why wouldn't I? he said. Aren't we dead long enough?

Oh Jesus, said Marie, the legs are hanging off me. Are ye watching the calves? I have a pair of calves on me like an Olympic sprinter.

Ah now!

They're having a great day in the graveyard! said Teresa.

Exactly so, said Brian. You might as well take it while it's going. We can just circle back and around as far as Drumeenaghadra, then back down into the village. Come on, Marie, for God's sake! It'll do you good.

Oh look, I don't know, she said. I might go back and rest up for a bit first. I don't know. Ye're putting me to shame!

Marie, come on! said Brian.

We'll see you later on so, said Teresa.

Okay, so not only did the two of them go and walk for another three hours, but then they spent another hour in the pub, drinking Smithwicks, and Marie sat in her room looking at the jungle wallpaper. She went to pee in the en-suite and as she sat there a cloud of plaster dreamily descended and settled on her head. It was eight o'clock—eight!—when they arrived back to the B&B. She tried to make light of it, she honestly tried.

I thought the two of ye were dead in a bog someplace! I thought we were going to have to get the mountain rescue out.

Oh stop, said Brian, flushed.

It was hard to make light of it. There was something not far from hatred in her eyes. The three of them went for steaks in the restaurant at the back of the pub. Marie was thinking, am I after letting myself get beat very easily here? Teresa was thinking, she's much prettier than I am, she always has been, am I only fooling myself? Brian was thinking, all they go on about in the women's magazines these days is sexual performance.

I'd nearly take the whole cow onto the plate, said Brian.

I wouldn't put it past you, said Marie, who had looked after half a bottle of decent Rioja in seven minutes flat.

It's great to see an appetite, said Teresa.

Very quiet and smirky in herself, thought Marie. What went on on that walk?

What had gone on on the walk was that Brian had talked sense to himself. Marie, he decided, was just too good-looking for him: he wouldn't have a hope in hell. Teresa, on the other hand, was at the back of the line when chins were being handed out and she had the eyes of a crow. Surely this might play to his advantage? Brian was versed in the cruel wiles of natural selection, he knew that the better-looking animal was the obvious choice, but natural selection is quick ignored when you've passed forty and you're masturbating into a sock the grey mornings in a one-bedroom apartment, lounge-diner-cum-kitchen.

And so it was that Brian and Teresa managed a semblance of flirtatiousness on the way back down to the village.

God, Brian, we're after getting some bit of fresh air into us today, said Teresa.

You'd nearly be driven wild with it, said Brian.

This, by his normal standard, by the normal old go of him, was richly provocative stuff. And suddenly she seemed to be walking very close. Her arm was touching off of his, and just the slight rubbery slap of Goretex on Goretex was enough to make him excited. Is that all it takes, he thought, the one ruby comment?

Some steak, said Brian.

It's great, said Teresa, it's done just right.

You can't top well-hung meat, said Marie, who was making shapes on her plate with fried onions. Waitress! Another bottle of that please.

Partying tonight, Mar! said Teresa.

Why the fuck not? said Marie. Has anyone change for the fag machine?

I didn't know you smoked, Marie, said Brian.

Many hidden talents, she said.

He sneaked a glance at Teresa then, who made a certain face which said: kid gloves here, pet, we'll leave her down easy. Brian was already becoming literate in Teresa's crow-like glances.

After the steaks, there was another painful hour in the pub. It was slow beer for Teresa and Brian, it was fast vodka for Marie. Teresa and Brian prepped each other carefully for the long opulent night that lay ahead.

Back at the St Ignatius of Loyola B&B, they said goodnight so, see you in the morning, bright and early! Brian went left for number nine, Marie and Teresa went right for six and seven.

Drink a glass of water when you go in, Mar, said Teresa.

Fuck off and rot, said Marie.

Half an hour later, Marie heard Teresa leave her room. She did not hear her come back again. She sat there with the light on, she felt headachey. She stood up on the bed and took the battery out of the smoke detector and lay down again and smoked fags.

First bus! She said it aloud.

She looked at the jungle scene on the wallpaper. Probably some-place like Mozambique, she thought. A nonsense jingle from an advert went through her head. Um Bongo. Um Bongo. They drink it in the Congo.

You don't mind if we wait a little while, do you? he said. Thanks, love. It's just that all this is very sudden for me, you know? But you ah… you can tell I'm pleased to be here with you anyway, can't you? There's no denying that!

There isn't, said Teresa, coyly.

Teresa decided that she was having a terrific time. This intimacy, she felt, was powerful stuff. Yes, she was greatly enjoying the whole experience but she would enjoy it all the more when she was at home on her couch, alone except for the cat, with the lights dimmed and a glass full to the brim and the late programme on Lyric playing low on the radio. Then she would savour it all truly.

In the kitchen, there was the sound of a kettle coming to the boil, of tea being made, of a pair of slippered feet crossing the polished lino.

I'm thinking of painting the walls blue, Minnie, said the tiny woman. What would you think, Minnie? A blue?

Listen, Teresa, said Brian. I'm totally prepared to give this another go. I have no problem whatsoever getting back up on the horse. Look it, will you come here to me? Oh this is magic.

See The Tree, How Big It's Grown

He turned to check his reflection in the window of the Expressway bus and some old quarehawk turned to look back at him. He appeared to be a man of about fifty. He did not appear to have set the world on fire. He looked beyond himself, and it had the look of South Tipp out there, lush and damp-seeming, with good-sized hills rising to the east, which would be the Comeraghs. He knew more about the hills than he knew about himself, but lush, yes, as if it was May, a savage growth that made each small copse of trees livid with bunched ferocity. The face seen dully in the window was a sad face, certainly, with a downcast mouth and emotional eyes, but it was strangely calm too. He took a glance south and found he was wearing an anorak long past its day, a pair of jeans with diesel stains caked into them and shoes straight off an evidence table. There was a bag, he noticed, in the rack overhead and he reached to take it down, breathing heavily. It was a Reebok holdall, scuffed and torn, and by no means a classy piece of luggage. He sat on the Expressway as it motored north through Tipperary this afternoon in the apparent summer with the bag in his lap. What kind of condition are you in at all, he wondered, when you wake up on a bus in the middle of countryside and you have no idea of who you are, or what your name is even?

The bus was quiet, with just a handful of sad cases thrown here and there, the elderly and the infirm, the free-pass brigade with their jaunty afflictions. He hefted the holdall, tested its weight. Come on now, what could be inside there? The head of John the Baptist? He opened it and with relief found just a sweatshirt and another pair of jeans. There was a box of fags, Bensons, and a yellow plastic lighter in a pocket of the jeans. There was a wallet in the other pocket, it held six hundred euro in cash and a scrap of paper folded over twice. The scrap of paper said 'Rooney's Auctioneers, 5pm.' It was at this point that he got the first of the tremors. This is what he would come to call them: the tremors. A tremor was when a flash of something came to him. The nature of this was visceral, more a feeling than a thought, and this first tremor came in the form of music, a snatch of music, five sad slow notes played on a recorder.

'Of course,' said an old fella in the seat opposite, looking across. 'I have the bus pass myself, I'd be going up and down the country on a regular basis.'

'Is that right?' he said, and his own voice was a surprise to him, a husky baritone.

'Oh yes. I do be bulling for road, you see. And I find that the B&Bs these days are excellent value for money. They serve you a powerful breakfast. And at this stage, most of the rooms have tea and coffee making facilities. And the cable as well. You can be watching Sky News.'

'I see.'

'And where'll you stay above?'

'The chances are,' he said, 'I'll be in a B&B myself.'

'Very good!' said the old fella, as if this was the best decision a man could ever hope to make.

There were certain pieces of information available. He knew, for example, that the course of Irish history was besmirched with treacheries and suppressions. He knew this because in some foggy classroom at the back of his mind he had been made to read it aloud to the rest of the children, despite or maybe even because of his terrible stammer. T-t-t-the course of I-I-Irish history is b-b-b-besmirched… You wouldn't likely forget the treacheries and suppressions after that.

The old boy looked over again, with rheumy eyes and gummy mouth, and he winked:

'Listen, there's every chance now we'll get in before five. You'll be able to get down to Rooney's, get a hold of them keys.'

'Do you reckon?' he said, and there was more than a sliver of fear in him.

'Ah we'll be in before five easy.'

A childish notion came. He thought that maybe he had died, and was in limbo, and that this old boy was some manner of gatekeeper. He shucked himself free of this sensation as best as he could, looked out the window: gloom floated down from morbid hills. The Expressway passed through a village, really more of a crossroads than a village, just a collision of a few byways and houses, a shop and, finally, a pub. As the bus passed by this establishment, the eyes nearly came out of his head. Was this, he wondered, a clue as to the character of the individual? He swivelled in his seat and looked desperately back down the road as the pub went out of view again. The throat was after going pure dry. He straightened himself and cast a wary glance across the aisle.

'He's making good time today,' said the old fella.

'He is.'

A bigger town announced itself with garden centres and D-I-Y warehouses and a large sign in the middle of a new roundabout that read:

BULMER'S CIDER WELCOMES YOU TO CLONMEL

'He's sucking diesel today,' said the old fella. 'Twenty to five!'

'Faith, he is,' he said.

Taking the Reebok holdall, he stood as the bus eased into the bleak station and he made a whistling attempt at nonchalance.

'Listen to me,' said the old fella, 'the best of luck to you now with everything. Something tells me you might have done a good deal here. And don't mind what the crowd below are saying.'

'Thanks very much,' he said, and he stepped off the Expressway and into the mysteries of Clonmel.

He wasn't long getting directions to Rooney's—Davitt Street, first left—and he wasn't long noticing that it was beside a small pub name of The Dew Drop Inn. He had a few minutes to spare, and there was a strange draw from this place, a magnet drag. The next thing he knew, he was inside at the counter, in the dank half-light, throwing the holdall down to his feet and putting his elbows up on the bar.

'What'll it be?' said the young one behind the bar.

'Pint b-bottle of B-Bulmer's,' he said, 'and a b-b-baby Powers.'

It appeared that he knew full well what he was doing in this type of situation. There was a bottle put down in front of him, and a pint glass filled with ice, and the small whiskey appeared as a cheerful companion. He made short work of this order, and he started to feel somewhat philosophical. What, after all, he said to himself, is an identity? Surely it is only a means of marking yourself out in time. And what is time in itself, only an arbitrary and entirely illusory system designed to remind us of death? To separate us from the eternal present enjoyed by the beasts of the fields. So why need you bother with either one, when you have the bones of six hundred euro in your fist, and a fag lit in the corner of your mouth? The five o'clock news came on the radio. It said Orla was missing since March 14th and the one clue for investigators was a red baseball cap.

'That'll be me,' he said to the young one, and she responded with a lazy smile and a stretching movement like a cat would make. There might be sport to be had in this place yet.

He strode in the door of Rooney's like a man who owned the rights to the whole of love. There was another young lady there, neat behind her desk, with a poignant mouth and agreeable knees.

'Good afternoon,' he said. 'I had an appointment for five?'

'Oh,' she said. 'It must be Mr Tobin, is it?'

'Correct.'

'Mr Tobin,' she explained, 'Mr Rooney is actually out at present. He is showing a pig operation in the direction of Knockbawn, but listen now, I have the keys and the lease here for you.'

'Outstanding.'

'The money has cleared. Everything is ready to go. All you have to do is sign your name. So if you'd like to take a seat, you can have a quick read through and make sure everything is in order.'

'I will,' he said. 'I'll take the w-weight off my feet.'

He felt that he was doing very well. His manner was charming, and if he didn't look exactly dapper, than at least he had a benevolent aura. Unfortunately, he noted, there was a smell of drink off him, which was something he would have to watch, but still and all he was presented with the necessary document. The lease shook a little as he read through it. It turned out he was after buying a chipper in Clonmel.

With the keys swinging, he set off into a most pleasant evening: the town swooned with glow, like a back-lit ale. He searched out No. 15a McDermott Street, which turned out to be no more than a hundred yards around the corner from Rooney's. After some trial and error with the keys, he managed to get the shutters up and the door opened and he crossed the threshold into a new era for both himself—Mr R.K. Tobin, apparently—and for the Uptown Grill.

So what do you do? What do you do when you wake up on a bus in South Tipp, and you don't know who you are, or where you're going, and the next thing you're inside in an auctioneers being presented with keys and then you're stood in the Uptown Grill, which is fourteen foot long by ten wide and contains a large deep fat fryer, a griddle, a glass-doored fridge, a full stock of supplies, a counter and a cash register? What do you do?

You start peeling spuds.

It quickly became clear that R.K. Tobin was not without some experience in the catering trade. The operation of the Uptown Grill didn't seem to faze him in the slightest. He wasn't in the door a half hour and he had wire baskets of nicely cut chips waiting for the fryer, he had the burgers battered, he had the haddock in breadcrumbs, and the potato cakes rolled, he had a griddle full of onions frying up nice and slow, releasing their sweetness to the air. Everything was waiting for the off, and as he worked he whistled a selection of show tunes from the early 1950s: 'If I Knew You Were Coming I'd A Baked A Cake', 'Cherry Pink And Apple Blossom White', 'Moon River'. His domestic arrangements, as it turned out, were all to hand, for he had climbed a greasy stairway out back and found a room above the chipper, same size, with a sink, a couch, a half bottle of Cork gin and a selection of golf magazines. He felt utterly alive with entrepreneuri-al swagger, and who was to say he wouldn't be taking up the golf himself? He brought the gin down with him as he prepared to open up for the teatime crowd. It just seemed like the thing to do.

Business came in fits and starts but overall it didn't seem a bad trade. It was steady enough through to seven o'clock, then you had lads late from work coming in for feeds, then a good crew around half-nine or ten in severe need of soakage. Quiet moments, he took a hit of gin from under the counter, looked out the door, saw the town fall away down the slate rooftops of terraces, turn into farm-land and fields, melancholy hills. The light was pleasing—a softness to it—and there was an amount of birds, though he did not know the names of birds.

How much did he know? You could say he had the broad strokes of things. He was only too well aware that he was an Irishman. He had a fair idea about the kind of lads who were coming in for burg-ers and chips: ordinary fellas, big eaters, red in the face from wind, hands like the buckets off JCBs, you'd imagine pulmonary disor-ders, midnight visitations. They were polite enough, made a certain amount of small talk. Nobody questioned or made direct comment on the fact of a new proprietor at the Uptown, but they were not unwelcoming of the stranger. One chap left a newspaper on the counter, which let him know he had a Tuesday on his hands. Somehow, this came as no great surprise. He had a quick look through the paper: odd, as if he knew things and at the same time, did not know. The way that a cow looks at you in the moonlight. A cow will incline its head to one side, and it'll stare at you with big wet eyes, as if it is sure it has seen you somewhere before but can't quite place you. This is the way he was reading the paper. Captains of industry, streels of girls at dinner dances, young lads hurling, planning applications, weddings, births, deaths. All of it was strange but familiar.

According to a notice on the door, the Uptown closed early on week nights, at eleven bells, and stayed late the weekends. He was-n't going to argue with that and at eleven o'clock, he closed up and took to the quiet streets for a breath of fresh air. There was a spit of misty rain falling, which was nice after the heat of the fryer, and even at eleven o'clock there were still some flecks of daylight in the far western sky. It was May, alright, he'd been bang on the money there. He stood smoking outside a department store, cool as a breeze but when he looked in at the window display, he was hit by another tremor, and this one nearly laid him out. It was the mannequin of a lady that did it, she was got up in the latest gear, some kind of suede outfit, and the way the mannequin's face was set was kind of… off, kind of twisted. It was set in a kind of drunken leer. The brown, wavy hair falling to the shoulders just so, the green belligerent eyes, the suede jacket, the leer—he had seen this look before. It was the mother.

They are walking down College Road. It's the night-time. She is still a young woman, with a child on either side of her. He would be the younger by a year or two, he might be seven years old. He has her by one hand and the other child, it has to be Denis, he has her by the other. She can barely get along the street, she lurches, drags them towards the railings. It's late, on a summer's night, and he has a bag of groceries in his hand. They mustn't have had the tea yet. The woman can't walk, she's crying, then she's laughing. She has a large brown bag with chips wedged under her arm, the vinegar is oiling the paper, and she almost drops it on the pavement as she misses her step.

'Mam,' he says, 'would you m-mind the chips, would yuh?'

The tremor passed on its way—down over the terraces of the town it went, away into the melancholy hills—and he bolted for the first pub he could find. By luck, it was quite a pleasant lounge bar and a hand-written notice on the door shakily announced that a pass-the-mike session was in progress. Pint bottle of Bulmers, b-b-b-baby Powers, times two, times three, and suddenly it was past midnight, and he was in flying form. There was a chap had a Casio keyboard and he was playing accompaniment to anybody who'd sing. A mike was passed around the dim-lit lounge, left and right, left and right, now who has the bar of a song for us? A woman called Mairead got up and smoothed down her good blouse and did an outstanding version of 'Wind Beneath My Wings'. The landlord, a man called Johnny—big sentimental face on him—came out over the bar and launched into 'The Day Billie Joe McAllister Jumped Off The Tallahatchie Bridge'.

'You'll learn a new one yet, Johnny!' somebody shouted, and everybody laughed.

Pint b-bottle, please. Someone called Bob sang 'The Black Hills Of Dakota', and wasn't asked to do another. After a while it got maudlin. A lad called Michael Russell was asked to sing, and he sang 'The Summer Wind', because that was some man called Coughlan's song and half of the place couldn't handle this at all, the man of the Coughlans was only a month in the ground.

'Fifty-two years of age!' cried Mairead.

Left and right, left and right, pass the mike.

'What about this gentleman here? What's your own name, sir?'

'Am… R-R-Richard,' he said.

'Will you sing one for us, Rich?'

'Ah stop!'

'Ah come on now, Richie!'

Where it came from, he did not know but he took that mike and he stood up square and he closed his eyes. He wasn't sweet—you couldn't say that—or melodic, no, but he was as big-voiced as they come, pure loud, a most powerful set of lungs. He sang 'Eternal Flame' by The Bangles.

'… cloh-ose yur eyes… gimme yur hand… darlin'… do you feel mah heart beat-iin'… do you unnerstan'… do you feel the PAAII-INN… am I own-lee dreeeamin'… or is this BURNIN'… an ee-ternal FLAME…'

There were people up off their stools howling for more. He pulled out a big one and let it rip—'Crying' by Roy Orbison. He made a fair reach for the high notes even. From the corner of his good eye, he threw a shine in the direction of the lady Mairead. There didn't seem to be a husband in tow.

'It's hard to unnn-erstan'… how the touuuuuccch of yur haaan'… can star' me cryin'… cry-aye-ah-han… an' now ahm ohhh-furrrr yuh-hooooooo…'

There was no doubt about it but he had a big future ahead of him at the pass-the-mike session in Keogh's Lounge Bar on Clancy Street of a Tuesday night. They asked him to do a third one, but he said no, no, firmly. You got to know when to hold 'em, and know when to fold 'em.

And yes, one good eye. He was only walking away from Keogh's when it struck him that he was half-blind. Leftie was firing blanks. He had a look up at the moon to be sure and he realised that the peripheries were indeed mightily skewed. So. The clues were starting to come in. He was an R.K. Tobin, call him Richie. He had the lease of a chipper in Clonmel. He'd had a mother a demon drunk, and a brother by the name of Denis. He was half blind, and something told him there had been an accident, and he had got money from it, which was now down to less than six hundred euro. He knew his way around the inside of a deep-fat fryer and home, for now, was a small unkempt room with a couch and a sink.

When he got there, he unscrewed the bottle of Cork gin and got good and familiar with it. He had the broad strokes of things and he knew that he had been drunk many thousands of times, mostly on account of the heebie jeebies. It was through no fault of his own but he was simply not the sort of man who was comfortable in the nighttime. He was familiar with the motions of alcohol. The elevations of mood were no news to him, nor the sudden dips. He knew what it was like to drink big in small towns—it was hard work sometimes, you had to have the same good time over and over again.

He picked up a golf magazine, then another, then noticed a magazine near the bottom of the pile that did not seem to be in any way, shape or form about golf. It was in fact a pornographic title and as he flicked through it, sipping at the gin, he discovered its theme. It was about women who dressed up by wearing animal tails. There was mail order, even, where you could send off for a horse's tail attached to a belt. Now maybe he was an innocent man for fifty, but this was news to him and there in the grim room, at two in the morning, it became an intense agitation. He got up off the couch and began to pace.

'Is this what it's all about now?' he shouted. 'Is that what's supposed to be going on around the place? Somebody's mother or somebody's daughter? Hah? Going around a kitchen in a horse's tail? Stood over a pan of sausages? Hah?'

He caught sight of the old quarehawk reflected in the window, pacing and ranting, and that shut him up lively. He turned off the light and lay down on the couch. He drew the malodorous anorak over his head. An unquiet sleep came. There were images full of dark portent, images of mountains and still water. It was an enormous relief when he woke to grey light in the window. He went immediately downstairs—though it was just gone five in the morning—and he got busy sorting out the grease traps. He looked out onto the street and it was familiar but odd, as if streets were running into the wrong streets, as if the hills were wrong, and the sky at a crooked slant, it was the amalgam place of a dream out there. A tremor arrived with the rise of the morning.

This student has been coming around Wednesdays for three or four weeks now. He is doing a project about low-income families. Richie think it's a disgrace, this fella is just a snoop, but his mother and father put up with it because they're bored, is what it is, because they're on the wagon, and they'll talk to just about anybody to escape the monotony. The student has all these daft bloody questions. Tonight it's about God and Mass and all that.

'Do you go to Mass yourself, Mrs Tobin?'

'Sometimes,' she says. 'Not that I believe that much in Jesus and stuff but it's just lovely sometimes, you know, if there's a choir and the way things are said.'

'The ritual, you mean,' he says. 'It's the ritual of the thing you admire?'

'Yeah.'

'And what about yourself, Mr Tobin?' he says. 'Do you have beliefs?'

'I don't know, really. I mean if you're asking me do I believe in miracles and walking on water and bread and fishes, I couldn't look you in the face and say oh I do, yeah. But if you're asking me when we're dead do we just lie around and rot in the ground like cabbage, well, I don't know that I believe that either.'

'And what about you, Richard?'

'Oh don't be asking him,' says the Da. 'Richie's a fucking pagan.'

He put a mop to the floor of the chipper. There was some relief in laying the suds down, squeezing the mop out in the wringer of the bucket, taking the suds up again. The day had arrived into Clonmel like a morbid neighbour, dour and overcast, the sky was low and dense, it was close in. As he swung the mop back and forth across the linoleum, things started to come apart altogether. He would begin to get a clear image, then somebody would drop a rock into the middle of the pool. Tremors queued up.

'Ah stop it for fuck sake,' he said.

But it's the Ummera Wood, he's fifteen years old and pustular, a hank of hair and hormones, and Denis is a year or two older. They're bush drinking—naggins of vodka. They sneak up on her quiet and she freaks out and screams, then laughs with relief 'cause she knows them—Denis and Richie. The three of them sit around drinking, and she's slagging them off because they're younger than she is. They drink the vodka. Denis gets quiet and moon-faced for a while, then he strikes up, he says Linda would you snog Richie, would yuh? Fuck off, she says, he's only a baby! Snog me so, he says. Nah, she says, you're too fucking ugly! And he has her by the hair then and she's down on the ground. What are yuh crying for, he says, we're only having a mess? And he's on top trying to screw her and Richie kneels down and puts his in her face and he says b-bite me and I'll fucking b-b-bate yuh.

He peeled spuds. He made batter for the burgers. He rolled out the potato cakes. He filleted the fish. He wondered where Denis had got to, and then he saw him: he was on his back underneath a Subaru Legacy at a garage outside a small town on a trunk road to Cork. He was covered in oil and diesel, there was junk everywhere, tarpaulin piles, dead Fiestas, tyres and wrenches, scrap iron, and Denis found that life was very hard sometimes because you cannot take a spanner to it.

(And love is very hard to do.)

Richie locked up the chipper for a while and he walked through the town to clear his head of all the crap that was building. He would stay in Clonmel for a time at least, nobody seemed to know him here—they say God looks after drunks and children. He walked to the town's far edge and there in the small garden of a house on a new-build estate, he saw a boy and a girl holding hands and crying and he went to them. He said, what's the matter? The dog is dead, she told him, and he asked the dog's name and she said the dog was called Honey, we had to bury Honey. He said I know a song about Honey and he sang the old Bobby Goldsboro number. A mother appeared at the front door, arms folded, thin smile, and he made a move back towards the centre of the town.

It was coming to life just then. Trim old ladies busied along towards the shops. Men were going into the ESB to talk about bills and easi-payment plans. He hummed to it all as he walked and then he thought that maybe if you tried hard enough you could transmit the thing itself out into the world and each time he passed somebody new he said lightly under his breath just the single word 'love', he said it to the postman and he said it to the guard, he said it to the old ladies and to the cats on the walls. The sun was making a good effort to come through the low banks of cloud; traffic streamed down for the new roundabout. Five sad slow notes played on a recorder. It was turning into June.

Animal Needs

Meadowsweet Farm is perhaps not the place you have prepared for. There is no waft of harvest to perfume the air. There is no contented lowing from the fields. These are not happy acres. Meadowsweet Farm is put together out of breeze blocks, barbed wire and galvanised tin. The land is flat and featureless. There are sawn-off barrels filled with rancid rainwater. A snapped cable cracks like a whip and lifts sparks from a dismal concrete yard—the electrics are haywire. The septic tank is backed up. The poultry shed is the secret torture facility of a Third World regime, long rumoured by shivering peasants in the mountain night. Desperation reigns, and we hear it as a croaky bayou howl. There is a general sensation of slurry.

John Martin stalks the ground, with a five-litre tub of white paint spattering a trail behind him. He pulls up short and considers a gate and decides to give it a quick undercoat, and does so. He nods to himself, acknowledgement of a job at least begun. There was an offer on the five-litre tubs, and hasty streaks of white are showing up all over Meadowsweet Farm this morning. He is painting gates and fences and breeze-block walls, barrels, sheds, pallets—if it stands still, he paints it. This is a brilliant white that will glow eerily after dark. It's as though he's preparing for an airlift evacuation. He fetches his tool box from the 4x4 and storms the poultry shed. He takes out a screwdriver and has another go at the fuseboard and suffers a mild shock. It leaves a silvery tingle all down his right arm, and to shake this feeling he rotates the arm several times through the air: a

rock star guitarist, with an audience of fowl. He goes outside again
and puts three lengths of ply across a muddy pathway. He paints
another bit of wall. He fetches the hard-wire sweeping brush and
goes through the yards, grimly janitorial. You'd swear that royalty
was coming and in a sense, it is: the woman from the Organic
Certification Board is on her way. He gets a cloth and a basin of
water and goes out to the road, where the Meadowsweet Farm sig-
nage has lately been erected—cheerful yellows and reds, a cock
crowing against a blue Iowan sky—and he wipes it down. He drags
some fertiliser bags out of a ditch and piles them for a bonfire. He
goes up to the house and into the kitchen and he eyeballs his wife
and he says:

'Mary? I'll ask you again. How many times did you come?'

This is no rosy-cheeked farmer. This is a gaunt and sallow man,
long-armed, with livid, electric hair.

'Fuck off,' says Mary.

He stands in the middle of the kitchen floor, with his feet planted for strength, and his neck warily hunched. He is watchful and
tense, five foot eleven of peeled nerves.

'All I'm saying is get it out in the open. Can't we talk about it
now, while she's at playschool? How many times, Mary? I swear I
won't hold it against you.'

She looks up from the computer. She scrunches her eyes tightly
shut and then opens them again hopefully, as if by mercy he might
have disappeared. It all reduces down to this thin sour broth: you
open your eyes and there's a nutjob on the floor in front of you.

'Why are you doing this? Haven't you enough to be doing outside? Do this much for me, John, okay? Turn around. And *fuck off.*'

Wounded, his mouth a grey slit, John Martin goes again into the
weather, and a filthy breeze has worked itself up, and he retreats to
the shelter of the chicken shed. Poultry management is no joke at the
best of times. You would be amazed what can go wrong. At present,
it is the heating. He has not been able to regulate the heat for five
days, and the shed is like Zaire. Unaccustomed to the luxury of such
warmth, the chickens have been unpleasantly lively but this seems
to be subsiding now to a kind of rattled exhaustion. They screech

and gasp in a terrible, grating way.

'Will ye ever shut up?' he says, and he wipes sweat from his brow. 'Please!'

This is Meadowsweet Farm in its fourth year. Previously, it was known only as Dolan's, her father's place, until he had a massive stroke, which was much deserved. All that was left of the Dolans then was Mary. They hadn't exactly been ringing the bells above in Sligo, so they thought, why not? People said from the start there was going to be a problem with the chickens. They were an expensive, high-faluting breed. People laughed at the idea of artichokes, too, and muttered knowingly the second September, the time of the artichoke famine. Orders have been slow enough coming in on the computer at Meadowsweet Farm. This is a scatter of acres outside the town of B____. There are both organic and traditional operations in the area. There are crisis levels of debt. There is alcoholism and garrulousness and depressive ideation. There is the great disease of familiarity. These are long, bruised days on the midland plain. People wake in the night and shout out names they have never known. There is an amount of lead insult among the young. The river is technically dead since 2002. There is addiction to prescription medications and catalogue shopping. Boys with pesticide eyes pull handbrake turns at four in the morning and scream the names of dark angels. Everybody is fucking everybody else.

An engine subsides in the yard outside. John Martin shakes himself alive and thinks no, Jesus, she can't be here already. He scurries to the yard but it is not the woman from the O.C.B. It is the grey Suzuki van. It's Frank Howe!

Howe steps out of the van, displays his palms in a gesture of openness and shucks the cuffs of his jacket.

'What about you, Big Man?' he says.

Howe is from the north and has crude animal intelligence. He can smell weakness and need. He steps across the greasy, puddled yard, and he kicks the fire-snapping cable from his path. John Martin raises a trembling hand to stop him.

'Frank,' he says. 'I'm going to ask you to clear out of here now. And I'm not going to ask you twice.'

He takes a wrench from the ground and holds it in threat above his head. He assumes an attack stance.

'Easy, killer,' says Howe. 'Is that one of mine?'

Frank Howe sells combination socket wrench sets at the markets. He also sells copies of Rolexes, pirate DVDs, illicit growth promoters and directions for dog fights. He stands calmly smiling in the Siberian wind. He chews on a scabbed knuckle. His black leather sports coat has its collar turned up. His peanut-shaped head is shaved to bristles. He has put the hours in on the sunbed. He can be no more than five foot two inches tall.

'It's too soon,' says John Martin. 'Oh it's too fresh, Frank! Fuck off out of here now lively.'

'She inside?'

'I'm warning you!'

'You'll warn nobody, John. We're as well to get that clear for a start. Put the wrench down and come in and talk to me like a good man.'

Mon, a gude mon. Howe strides like a six-footer into the poultry shed. He drags out a pail and sits on it. He sets his face sternly, and hovers his fingers in the air: a kestrel waiting to swoop, or a concert pianist poised to begin.

'I am a man,' he says, slowly, emphasising each word.

Aaah… ohmmm… a… mon.

'And she,' says Howe, 'is a woman.'

A wummun.

John Martin considers cranking shut the slide-door. He considers taking a leap through the air and beating Howe all about the head with the wrench. He could wrap the body in opened sacks and drag it to the prep area and put it through the mincer, piece by piece, mix it with the mix for the meatballs, flavour with coriander and lime, put it out to the farmers' markets, Thai-style.

'You,' says Howe, 'are a man.'

He winks, appreciatively, at John Martin.

'And Madge,' he smiles, 'is a woman.'

Howe shuts his eyes and takes a small bow.

'End of story,' he says. 'I had a go off yours. You had a go off mine. If you like we can put four crosses on St Jarlath's pitch and nail ourselves to them. Or we can get on with us lives and forget all about it. Be friends still. Look. Come over tonight, John, bring herself. We'll have a few drinks and relax, for Godsake. Is all I'm saying to you.'

'You're trying to destroy my family,' says John Martin.

The heads of the chickens twist from each to the other, like the crowd at Roland Garros. Howe stands and kicks the pail aside. He shrugs. He pushes past John Martin in the doorway and heads for the van.

'Take your ease, John,' he says. 'I'll give yez a tinkle later on, soon as I'm done in Shinrone.'

John Martin walks into the fields of the farm. It is all around him, and there is a vague hissing at its edges, as in a sour dream. She is due for twelve and the place is an out-and-out disaster. Meadowsweet Farm is a concern on the brink. The O.C.B. runs a tight ship, and if they cannot get on board, they might as well turn the place over for sites. Be done with it. He notes a rusted gate and fetches a scraper and opens a fresh tub of the white paint and rinses out a brush under the tap in the yard. He sets to. Madge Howe is an attractive lady but mad. The glazed look, the grey tongue. There is going to be hell to pay. What was he thinking?

He takes rust off the gate. A fine mist of copper-coloured particles lifts into the air and causes him to sneeze. He cannot shake the fear that his daughter has been permanently damaged. She is a spaced out kind of child at the best of times, but she has gone even deeper into herself since. Fear is a black wet ditch on a cold night. It is hard to claw yourself out, your fingers slip in the loam. He puts an undercoat on the gate. He takes a couple of fertiliser bags out of a hedge. He cannot even think about going to have a look at the few cattle. There is a white nervous sky, and magpies are everywhere on patrol, stomping around, like they own the place. He takes one of the phones from his pocket and puts in a call to Noreen.

'Can I come over?' he says

'Oh John,' she says. 'No way. I don't know how long he's going to be gone.'

'I can't stop thinking about you,' he says.

'Shut up!' she says.

'I want you now, Noreen.'

'I'm warning you!' she says.

'How long is he gone?'

'No.'

'Can we not chance it?'

'No.'

'I'm in love with you, Noreen,' he breathes it, a whisper, a husk on the breeze.

'Park on the L_____ road,' she says, 'and come over across by Tobin's field.'

He climbs into the 4x4. It'll be chancy on time but what are you going to do? The bayou howl, the bayou howl. He backs out of the yard, goes down the drive, turns onto the road. He will need to stop off in town to pick up condoms. He is in the thirty-seventh winter of his life. The other phone goes, the official line. Caller i.d. says 'mry'.

'What?'

'Where you goin'?'

'I've to head into town.'

'What for?'

'I've to get rope.'

'Pick up the dog while you're there'

'You're not serious, Mary? She's not!'

'What?'

'She's in *again*?'

'Yes.'

'Arra the fuck, since when?'

'I'd to drop her in this morning. She was bad. You were told this. You were in the back fields. I'm talking to a wall is what I'm talking to. She's ready since eleven. They rang. They said pick her up.'

'She's in *again*?'

Picking up the dog will not be straightforward. The pregnancy has been a nightmare, she's even been snapping at the child. When John Martin interfered with her supper one night, pushing it out of the way with his foot, she nearly took his face off. She is a fast-tempered spaniel bitch, high-bred, with taut nerves. He breaches the tearful peripheries of the town. He makes it through to the central square under a tormented sky; he parks. The vet's clinic is on one of the terraces that traipse from the square. There are feelings strong enough to overwhelm the physical laws. There are feelings that can settle in stone. There is an age-old malaise in the vicinity of this terrace. It has soaked into the grain of the place. The afternoons looking out on sheeting rain... The nights staring into the dark infinities... How would a place be right after it?

The vet's clinic, however, is ignorant of such desperation. It has by force of will and riches wiped it from the hard-drive. The clinic is styled in chrome and blonde wood, there are slate tiles and extravagant leather couches in a reception expertly wardened by a seething goddess of Slavic extraction: a limbre Svetlana. Matronly ladies on the couches nurse trembling small dogs: this time of morning, the vet's is poodle terrain.

'Hiya,' says John Martin. 'About the dog?'

'Name, please.'

'Martin. John Martin.'

'Dog name!' spits the ice queen.

'De Valera.'

She speaks into a headset. Clearance comes through and he is allowed access to the shimmering depths of the building. How the fuck much are vets making these days?

'Hiya John!'

A headful of tousled locks emerges from a doorway. The vet has a stevedore handshake and millionaire teeth. He is a tan, highlighted guy of maybe sixty five. Dev reclines on a space-age gurney. She wears an expression of sainted pain. She averts her gaze from John Martin. She has the look of a brittle heiress cruelly sectioned in the ripe years.

'Clearly, yes, it's a moody little thing we got on our hands,' says the square-jawed vet, and he flicks at his bleachy flop of hair.

'I imagine the pregnancy would be...'

'There are hormonal events, absolutely, but from what I've been told, things are cutting a little deeper with Dev. I've done bloods, they'll go for checks, and what can I say? We'll play wait-see.'

'And, eh...'

'Now maybe a lot of this stuff will resolve itself in the very near future.'

'Once she has the litter?'

'It should do an amount for her temperament, John, but even so I feel things have got to a stage where I'm going to prescribe an additional treatment. At least for the time being.'

'Oh?'

'To be sure to be sure. Belt and braces.'

He presents John Martin with a small white packet containing forty-eight sachets of K-9 Serenity.

'You sprinkle it on her dinner, just the one a day.'

'What is it, exactly?'

'It's an anti-depressant.'

'The dog is depressed?'

'It would seem so, John, yes.'

John Martin settles with glowering Svetlana; cash, as he no longer holds an account at the vet's. Dev's treatment costs about the same as a week in France. He is not in a position to grizzle about this, as he has a more pressing concern. De Valera is refusing to walk. He tugs on the leash, but there is venomous resistance. He tugs again, and she yelps. The matrons on the couches mutter. De Valera moans. He drags her across the slate tiles. He bends to pick her up and finds there is an unpredictable amount of spaniel to deal with, and the thought of the litter inside is queasy. On the street, she snarls at him. He has to hold her at arm's length to prevent blood being drawn. He puts her down on the pavement with more force than is necessary.

'For fucksake, Dev! Behave!'

An assault of fresh rain is carried slant-wise from the west. A tuneless brass band strikes up inside. Nervous agitation works like water on stone. It is a slow, steady dripping that can meet no answering force. Over time, it washes everything away.

With De Valera livid in the passenger seat, John Martin drives out the far side of the town. He stops at Lidl and pops in for some

German condoms. There is a twilight beach scene on the pack: a big blonde couple, arm in arm, up to their eyeballs in it by a dusk-marooned sea.

The town recedes in the rear-view mirror. He pulls onto the bare, desolate stretch of L_____ Road. He parks at the usual place. He is about to set off when Dev begins to rave and foam again. The dog might be heard, might draw prying eyes to this quiet place. He rips open two sachets of K-9 Serenity and sprinkles them on the floor in back—it is a greyish mica dust, and De Valera is drawn to it like love.

John Martin slips away, and cuts across by Tobin's field. He feels a familiar guilt—not two weeks previously, he had dosed also his daughter.

It was a Saturday evening, at the hotel bar. It was the usual run of things.

You'd do a few bits in town, and then hit back to D_____'s Hotel for a feed of drink. All the other couples would be around, all the old familiars. John and Mary Martin fell in as always with Frank and Madge Howe. Frank had been making cracks about it for months. He said they'll be talking, John, they'll be asking questions, mark my words. Who's with who, they'll say. He had brought it up, again and again, and it seemed less jokey each time. Then he took John Martin aside in the gents.

'What about it?' he said. 'Grown adults so we are?'

John Martin blushed, and chuckled, but Howe continued.

'No objections on our side,' he said. 'Sure yez could come on up after?'

John Martin tried to laugh it off but there was a tension. In the lounge, he told Mary, and she smiled and said:

'Arra. They're lively at least.'

'I don't think he's messing any more, Mary. I think he's full in earnest.'

'Sure what harm in it?' she said.

Then they were back in the front room of the terrace house the Howes were renting. Curry boxes everywhere, vodka and beer.

Frank was messing with the stereo and singing along, red in the face. Madge and Mary were skitting and whispering. Frank went up the stairs and came back down with a huge pile of sports jackets in bright colours.

'My new line,' he said, 'they're selling like hot dogs so they are.'

'Cakes,' said John Martin. 'Hot cakes.'

'Will you do a spot of modelling for me, Johnnie boy?'

And the two of them paraded up and down, in the jackets, and pushed the sleeves up, play-acting.

'Crockett and Tubbs!' roared Madge.

And 'The Best of The Eagles' was put on and they all danced and Frank said, what about it, Tubbs?

Then it blurred, and Frank and Mary walked out of the living room.

'Come on, John,' said Madge, and she grabbed the car keys, 'we'll head for yours.'

You imagine the whole wife-swapping business would take four decisions but really it only takes three.

He moves across the low dip of the bottom fields, rat-faced with need and longing. His long arms swing with intent, one then the other in slow pendulum. He mutters onto his breath as he walks. He climbs over the fence and onto the Flaherty land. An old horse they keep, spared the knackers out of sentiment, regards him with due suspicion, with a knowingness, and returns to its cud with patent disgust. The Flaherty house arises, and he squints towards the yard to make sure there is no Rover jeep there. Lit with nerves and excitement, priapic in the sour light of noon, he approaches the kitchen window, and taps, and she comes to it at once. He blows a fog onto the pane. She unlatches the door, with a scowl, and he steps inside, with a quick squint over his shoulder, and he goes for her.

'Back off!' she says.

'What are you talking about, Noreen? You told me come!'

The long arms swing out, beseeching.

'I made a mistake. You can take off from here now and don't mind the old shite talk. He's only gone in for diesel.'

'Don't be telling lies! You wouldn't have told me come if it was diesel. I have yokes.'

He shows the condom packet.

'You come around here sniffing like a mutt!' she hisses, and begins to cry. 'I made the mistake before, I won't make it again! Out!'

'An hour ago, Noreen! Park by the L_____ Road, you said. Cut across by Tobin's field. Am I making this up?'

'You're under stress, John. This isn't the answer! Just go, okay?'

'I see,' he says, 'I see what you're trying to do here. You're trying to turn it back on me. You're…'

The Rover jeep pulls into the yard. Noreen freezes, then goes into convulsions, her breath rolls through her system in heavy gulps, and she grips the fridge to keep the feet beneath her. John Martin almost smiles: ah not this old dance again. From the window, he can see big Jim Flaherty pounding across the yard. This Flaherty is no gentle giant. He is carrot-topped, with a hair-trigger temper, and a specific distaste for John Martin on account of a previous situation involving lambs. Now he fills the kitchen door. Now he lays his eyes on John Martin.

'Jim! The very man. I was only in looking for you. What I wanted to know, Jim, was had you the loan of a wire-cutters? I've only an auld bevel-edge below, no use at all for the job at hand. It's a new boundary I'm putting up for the chickens, give them some bit of a run at least. They'd reef themselves if I went at it with the bevel-edge. What I'd need would be a semi-flush. Of course it's a last-minute job, as usual. I have herself from the O.C.B. coming around to me. Today, would you believe, and I'm still at it. So would you ah… would you ah… The last minute man! Dancing with the devil in the pale moonlight.'

'God, John, a semi-flush? I don't know. I… *don't* think so. No, John, no. I'm afraid not. Apologies. Nothing I can do to help you out there. Have you thought of Mangan, or Troy?'

'True, I suppose, I could nearly ah… I could nearly… I could knock in, I suppose?'

'You could, John. Especially given they'd be five miles nearer to you. Given they'd be neighbours.'

'I ah…'

'And tell me, by the way, while we're at it,' and Jim Flaherty takes a dainty step back, a little dancing step back, and he blocks off the door with an arm to the jamb, an arm with the reach of a mid-sized crane. 'Tell me, John. Where you parked?'

'Oh, I ah… I left it down by L_____ Road. Actually.'

'I see. You decided to park twelve hundred yards away. At a spot that is hidden from the open view. I see.'

'Listen, anyway, folks, I'll knock away out of it. I'll see ye.'

'I'll tell you now, John, we can do it easy or we can do it hard. Which way would you want it to be?'

'Easy.'

'Good man. So how long have you been sleeping with my wife?'

'Jimmy!' she cries. 'This is crazy talk!'

'Noreen, love, would you ever go upstairs and lock yourself into the bathroom and put the key out under the door for me? I'll deal with you in due course. John, you might take a seat by the fireplace, please.'

Noreen trots for the stairs. John Martin sits down on a straight-backed chair. Jim Flaherty takes a length of rope from beneath the sink. He comes across the floor, smiling softly in a pair of well-pressed denims.

'I was wondering all along who it was,' he says, 'but you know I never once thought it'd be a Clare man! Then again, you're nearly always surprised at what looks up at you out of the trap.'

He winds the rope gently but firmly around John Martin's thin waist, around and around, and he knots it quickly and precisely. He takes a clean, ironed tea towel from a drawer and presents it to the bound farmer.

'I want you to use this as a gag, John,' he says. 'It'll stop you swallowing your tongue.'

'And what, am… what am… precisely?'

'What I'm going to do, John, is I'm going to dislocate your shoulder. It'll give you something to remember the day by.'

Sometimes, in the slow drag of winter, terrible sounds will pierce the calm of the midlands air, and we look up, and our brows gather in knit nervous folds, but we persuade ourselves that it is otherwise, that these are not the cries of humankind. But we know! In our hearts, we know.

John Martin comes back across the bottom fields, walks with a drop-shouldered jerk, and he's had thumps in the mouth as well, and they took teeth with them. Oh the terrible spittle of revenge that formed on the grey lips of big weeping Jim Flaherty! But he must leave it go. The woman from the O.C.B. is due ten minutes since. He gets back to the 4x4. De Valera is gone apeshit on the K-9 Serenity.

'I swear to God to you, John, I didn't! Not at all. Not even close.'

'How many times, Mary?'

Half eleven in the morning, the Sunday after the Saturday, and she stood there, and she lied to him! He was sat in the kitchen trying to eat a sausage sandwich. And there is no bite to eat he likes better in the week than the sausage sandwich of a Sunday morning. And he couldn't eat it.

'No, honest to Jesus,' she said. 'It wasn't the same. It was just... different. All I wanted was to be back at our usual auld thing. Never again!'

He tried to believe her. He gripped himself inside and squeezed hard, and he felt a little better. He took a bite out of the sausage sandwich, chewed it, remorsefully, and shook another lash of brown sauce into it. He was man and boy a martyr to the brown sauce. His head wouldn't let him be.

'I'll ask you again,' he said. 'Did you come, Mary?'

He does not believe that his wife is a malicious woman. He is no fool and he knows that there are women who have malicious streaks. His mother, now, was a malicious woman, you could even say an evil woman. He would never forget the night he went into her room after she'd unbeknownst to him been with O'Donnell and the way she was lying on her stomach and the way she turned around to him and the way she kind of... *writhed*, is the only word, like a serpent, and the look that was on her face. Pure hate. But Mary, no, he didn't think she had that streak in her.

He had to believe her, somehow. There were walls in the house painted more often than Mary came, and he wanted to be sure it was her, not him.

He didn't know how he finished that sausage sandwich but by Jesus he finished it. Then he went out to the chickens. He walked through the yard. A Sunday, and he gave an impression of slitheriness, like a stoat.

Driving a 4x4 with a dislocated shoulder is no picnic, not when the white sear of the pain waters your eyes and blurs your vision. But it is nothing at all compared to driving a 4x4 with a dislocated shoulder while a manic-depressive spaniel, in manic phase, answerable only to the tides of the moon, makes repeated assaults upon the area of your crotch. Blood streaming down his face, raging against it all, tears streaming from the sheer physical agony, spitting teeth—it is in this state that John Martin pulls into the yard of Meadowsweet Farm. He is awaited there by his wife, and by the woman from the O.C.B.

Mary comes running.

'Oh Jesus!' she cries. 'Oh Christ! Oh Dev! Are you okay?'

'Hello there!' calls John Martin, and staggers from the jeep, and falls to his knees. 'I'm afraid I got caught up in the town. I'd a bit of am… a bit of an auld am… whatchacallit.'

The woman from the O.C.B., a tall, thin matron in a green wax jacket, takes a couple of nervous steps back.

'Bastard!' cries Mary Martin, and she runs screaming to the house, with the small howling dog in her arms.

The worst of it was that he had crushed two Valium into hot milk and then poured it into his crying child to conk her out. It was Madge's idea, and they were her tablets, but what kind of a father would do that? And for what turned out to be a five-minute special. And Madge lay there, for the rest of the night, yapping nonsense out of her, smoking her fags.

'That young miss will sleep now sweet as a dream for you, John, you have nothing to worry about there. These are the English Valium, you see, these are the Valium we used get all along. Until they starts making them below in Clonmel. Clonmel! They're not the same at all and I'm not the only one that's saying it. Honest to God, John, you might as well be eating Smarties. But I have an arrangement about the English Valiums with the man in the chemist, the man of the McCaffertys. Have you ever noticed, John, the way every single last one of the McCaffertys has the big teeth?'

He had never put down a night like it.

He came from a town himself, it wasn't as if he had background in poultry management. It was not a pleasant setup, not by any stretch, not when a smother of them would go on you, all the disease. There was a young fella in town wore one of the long coats with the badges and he was forever buttonholing John Martin with rants about cruelty. What about the quality of life, he'd say, getting himself all worked up. What about my quality of life, said John Martin. Do you think I'm outside in a palace?

The poultry shed was bad now. It was bad. But he had mixed feelings about the poultry shed. He had mixed feelings because it was the one place his daughter was calm, it was the one place she never cried out or skittered. She would pull at him to take her there and he'd go. She'd sit there on a pail in her red coat and it was like she was in a chapel.

He couldn't get it out of his mind all the following week. Slugging around the place, trying to look after chickens, and it haunting him. First thing in the morning, last thing at night. Madge was handsome but crazy, and he didn't need any more distractions. There was already the situation with Noreen. There was also the situation with Kelli Carmody at the sports centre, though that was most definitely over. Kelli was nineteen, for Christ's sake, and they are unpredictable as snakes at that age. He had changed the hours of his workouts to avoid her, and he fully intended to continue doing so. There is only so much a man's heart can take. He was still getting over Jenna. He knew whenever he saw her at the till in Lidl that he wasn't fully over her yet. And Yvonne, too, Yvonne Troy was a heartbreaker. So no, there would be no more messing, there would be no situation with Madge. Even if she did have legs that went up to Armagh.

The woman from the O.C.B. is polite but firm.

'No way, John. I mean, seriously,' and she half laughs. 'You're not even in the ballpark here. We have to maintain standards, you know?'

'I realise,' he says, through gritted teeth, because the pain is if anything increasing, 'that there needs to be an improvement in the poultry shed.'

The woman from the O.C.B. climbs into her jeep. She sits for a moment with her feet held out the door, and yanks off her Wellingtons, one then the other, and flexes her toes in the stockinged feet, then reaches in for the driving shoes. A slight colour comes into her cheeks from the exertion of this.

'I realise,' he says, 'that I need to regulate the heat and get a decent run marked off. I realise I need to invigorate the feed.'

She wears streaks in her hair and the faintest trace of lipstick and her left eye turns in slightly to regard a haughty nose. She isn't bad at all.

'John,' she says. 'This isn't really about the chickens.'

The child is home from school. She is at the upstairs window, utterly blank-faced, looking out at it all. She pulls the heavy curtain shut, tottering with the weight, and the room becomes dark as night. The heels of her trainers light up as she crosses to the bed. She climbs in and pulls the covers over her head to thicken the dark. She flashes her torch, on and off, again and again. It is night-time in a secret world. There are dancing bears on a frosty rooftop as the happy music plays. She walks the twinkling streets. The good witch waves from a high window. The postman cycles across the sky. She turns up the music still louder. A bulldog barks a yard of stars.

Last Days Of The Buffalo

An indisputable fact: our towns are sexed. Look around you. It's easy enough tell one from the other. Foley's town, for example, is most certainly a woman—just take in the salt of her estuarine air—but she's not a notably well-mannered or delicate woman. She is in fact a belligerent old bitch. You wouldn't know what kind of mood you'd find her in. And so he storms out, every afternoon, and slams the door after himself.

He walks the trace of a creek that takes him into countryside. Today the creek is particularly foul, there is either something very rotten in there or something very alive. Foley walks by and sniffs at it but he has no great interest. This is an enormous, distracted, heavy-footed creature we're dealing with. He's jawing on his thoughts. He's remembering the knockdown fights with his father in the street.

These are the dog days of summer. The country feels heavy. There's a lethal amount of growth and he's pollen-sick from it, Foley, the last of August pulses in his throat. He can see across the estuary to the malevolent hills of Clare. Do hills brood, as they say? Oh they sure do. Foley's massive hands are dug into the pockets of his outsized jeans and the hedgerows tremble with birds. Foley's eyes are watery, emotional, a scratched blue, and they follow the caked dry mud of the pathway. Along the verges there are wild flowers—pipewort, harebell, birdsfoot trefoil, grass of Parnassus, all so melodious sounding it would turn your stomach—and they bloom and shimmer for Foley but he won't give them the satisfaction.

His father sang 'Sean South of Garryowen'. His father sang 'Dropkick Me Jesus'. His father sang 'The Broad Black Brimmer Of The IRA'. A roof-lifting tenor the old fucker had and unquestionably a way with the ladies.

Dogs somewhere, and the bored drone of motorway traffic, distant, like the sound of a dull dream, also chainsaws.

And he walks the trace of the water, Foley, and he comes within the shadow of the cement factory. The grasses and reeds are dusted grey from the factory's discharge. This is the type of country that would redden your eye and Foley knows it all too well. He spent seventeen years at the Texaco out here—it was, for a time, an ideal confluence of beast and task.

At the start, it was just two pumps beside a dirty little kiosk for the till. Midwestern rain hammered down on the plastic roof. Electric fire, a kettle, a crossword and Foley might have been in the womb he was so cosy. He near filled the kiosk. He was prince of the forecourt. He knew the customers by name: the boys from the cement plant, the Raheen businessmen, the odd few locals. Foley was pure gab in those days. He'd talk shock absorbers, chest infections, four-four-two. He'd talk controversial incidents in the small parallelogram the Sunday gone. But word came through and there was quickly great change. Statoil bought out Texaco and the kiosk was bulldozed. An air-conditioned, glass-fronted store went up, with automatic doors and cooler units. Foley found himself with colleagues. The next thing they were squeezing him into a uniform and sticking a bright red hat up top. Then they started fucking about with croissants. Then they put in a flower stall and started selling disposable underwater cameras—the better, presumably, to document the coral reefs of the Shannon. Foley went to the supervisor.

'Come here I want you,' he said.

'Yes?'

'I want to get one thing clear,' he said. 'Just for my own information.'

'Yes?'

'Are we a petrol station? Or are we an amusement arcade?'

'I must say your tone is slightly…'

'Don't mind tone. Are we a supermarket?'

'Now listen…'

'What the fuck are we?' cried Foley. 'Are we Crazy Prices?'

'There's no need for your tone, I find it…'

'I'll give you tone!'

He lunged for him and that was that. Don't come around here no more, they told Foley, and it was the end of the seventeen years.

Foley was six foot five on the morning of his fourteenth birthday and half as wide again. This is the original brick shithouse we're talking about. He was a clown of a child. His father informed him daily he was fit for Fossett's. There wasn't a school jumper could be got in the town to fit him. The best his father could do was a chandlers on the Dock Road that stocked a heavy-duty v-neck designed for vast trawlermen sent to face the wrath of the Irish Box. Foley at fourteen wore it to face the Brothers. In cold weather, the rad in the classroom would seize up and to free its workings it needed to be hit a wallop and this became Foley's job. The teacher would roar down in a hoarse, booze-scratched voice:

'Foley! Hit that rad an auld slap, boy. You're good for something anyway, you big eejit.'

And he'd slug across the floor, Foley, and the other boys would do the Jaws music—dah-duh, daaaah-duh, daaaaaaah-duh—and he'd wind up the shoulder, take a swing at the thing with an opened palm and it'd gurgle back to life from the pure shock of force.

Quiet awe would swell in the classroom.

The shovelers call from the reedbeds but they could stand up on tippy-toes and sing Merle Haggard and Foley wouldn't pay the blindest bit of attention. He's thinking about the time he had the fucker down and a knee on his throat and he could have closed that windpipe lively but no, what possessed him but he let the bastard go.

He has been told he should try accentuate the positives. And certainly, it hasn't been Crapsville all the way. He has had small blessings. He has never, for example, had to journey through the regions of romance. That would have been on the rich side. Of course there are sugary men who will croon that love, at length, shines on each and all of us—woo-oooh! woo-oooh!—but no, thanks be to God, love never came next nor near Foley. Not that till he was twenty-six or twenty-seven, and six foot ten in the full of his growth, the big ape, not that he didn't maintain a glimmer of hope: maybe, oh just maybe... This was a young man listening to enough country and western music to believe just about anything. But he never tried to foretell the detail of it. He never tried to picture it actually come true. Was she really going to float down from the starry sky and put in an appearance on O'Connell Street some Saturday? Walk up to the big tank called Foley and tap him on the shoulder? Settle down and raise enormous children? It wasn't going to happen, and it never did, and it was sweet relief to give up on even the notion.

He walks on. There has been an unpromising start to the new season—two draws and a loss—and black squalls cross his brow when he thinks of the remarks that have been made. Do not say the wrong thing about Manchester United in the vicinity of Foley. Then the storm clouds will gather. Then you'd want to leave a wide berth. He wears the number seven jersey that says 'Cantona' on the back. It's the biggest size the mail-order people can do but still a tight fit. See him of an evening, sat on the corner stool, there in the shadows, with the dry-roasted nuts, and the pint glass like a thimble in his hand. It would go through you, if you were unfortunate enough to be in any way soft-natured.

He follows the creek, goes past the factory, and the creek begins to quicken once it rounds the bend that leaves Mungret behind. Ahead of him on the pathway there's a distraction. On the last high bank of the creek there are some boys gathered and as he approaches them he grows wary because he can see the shimmer of their gold in the afternoon sun. They wear streaks in their hair and dress shirts in bright colours. They have alert brows and startled eyes. There are six of them, no, seven, there's eight of them, count, nine? Travellers.

'Story, boss?'

'What's the story, big man?'

'Some size of a creature we've on our hands here, boys. Look it!'

They stand in a half-circle to block the pathway but they keep switching position, they keep dancing around the place, it's as though they're on coals, and their voices have hoarse urgency.

'Where you headed, sir?'

'Are you headed for the hills, I'd say?'

'Come here I wancha? Where do they keep you, do they keep you in a home?'

'What brings you out this way, sir? And what size are you at all, hah? If you don't mind me asking, like. You must be seven foot tall?'

'Tell me this and tell me no more. What size is the man below? The women must think it's Leopardstown.'

'Now listen,' says Foley. 'That's the kind of talk I won't abide.'

'It has a tongue!'

'Ah come here now and go easy. Where do you live, fella? Are you inside in the city? Are the Health Board looking after you?'

They move in closer, and the talk changes to a confiding tone.

'Listen. You'd do us a turn, hey? You see what it is, we're short a few yo-yo for a game of pitch 'n' putt below in Mungret.'

'Pitch 'n' putt my eye,' says Foley. 'You fellas are no more playing pitch 'n' putt.'

'You're calling us liars?'

A leader emerges. He spreads his arms like he's nailed to a cross and he looks to the sky in great noble suffering and he bellows from deep:

'Hold on, boys!'

It should have been obvious who the leader was. His shirt is of the richest purple and his hair is the most vivaciously streaked. His gold shimmers in the sun and he slaps a stick off the ground.

'Hold on, boys. What we're dealing with here is no old fool. You're right, sir. We are having nothing at all to do with the pitch 'n' putt. Truth be known, there is a tragedy we're dealing with. Martin here—the runt—Martin's mother is laid out below in Pallasgreen. Misfortunate Kathleen! God rest her and preserve her and all belongin' to her. And the situation we're after been landed in, through no fault of our own, we're short the few euro to wake her right. So help us out there, boss, will yuh? Martin is in a bad way.'

'I'm bad, sir,' says Martin. 'I am bad now. And I guarantee you there'll be prayers said.'

'Shush now,' says the leader, and again he slaps the stick off the ground, but Foley just smiles.

'Out of my way, gentlemen,' he says. 'I'm going to walk on through.'

The leader slaps the stick again and exhales powerfully through his nose.

'We're not getting through to you, hey? Put your hand in the pocket there and help us out, like.'

They dance around him again, they swap and jostle with each other, they have terrible static in them, but Foley doesn't move, and Foley doesn't speak. The leader comes a step closer.

'Who the fuck do you think you are?'

Foley smiles.

'Look,' he says. 'We're off on a bad footing. Can we not be civilised? Can we not calm ourselves? Look. I'll tell you what. Will you shake my hand?'

The leader smiles. Negotiations have been smoothed. He opens his face to Foley. He is a reasonable person.

'Of course,' he says. 'Of course I'll shake.'

Foley closes his hand softly around the boy's hand then and a cold quiver passes between them. It's the feeling in the hazel switch when it divines water, and it's the feeling that comes at night when a tendon in the calf muscle has a twitched memory of a falling step, and it's there too, somehow, in the great confluence of starlings, when they spiral and twist like smoke in the evening sky. Foley holds the boy's hand and the feeling sustains for a single necessary moment.

'You were born the fourth son in a lay-by outside Tarbert,' he says, 'and you'll die a wet afternoon in the coming May. The way I'm seeing it, a white van will go off the road at a T-junction. A Hitachi, if I'm seeing it right. And I can tell you this much, Bud—it ain't gonna be pretty.'

'What you sayin' to me? What you sayin' to me you fat fuckin' freak?'

The leader shucks his hand free and takes a step back, and the others step back too. Foley, arrogant now, draws a swipe through the air, as though he's swatting flies, and he walks on through. For a while the traveller boys follow and they taunt him from a distance but he knows they will not make the decision.

The creek dwindles to its outflow, and the estuary has an egginess, a pungency. The lethargy of swamp gives way to the slow momentum of the Shannon. From across the water, the hills of Clare look on unimpressed. You would be a long time impressing the hills of Clare. A path branches off from the creek and from here you can follow the river back into town and it's a weary Foley that turns onto the branching. Sweat pours from his armpits and stains the number seven shirt that says 'Cantona' on the back. Oystercatchers work the rocks, most efficiently, and the lapwings are up and gregarious, but Foley doesn't want to know. He limits his thoughts to each step as it falls. His heavy head lifts up now and then to find the town come closer, and still closer.

It is more difficult to look back. At the way Foley Snr would come home in the evening, take off his workboots, slap his fleshy paws together and do the hucklebuck in the middle of the floor. Twist the hips and pout the lips: ladies and gentlemen, a big hand now for the west of Ireland's answer to Mr Jerry Lee Lewis. He'd manhandle the missus. He'd make slurping noises at his supper. He'd bounce the big child on a giant's round knee.

'Is the water on? Have you the water on at all? How am I supposed to get washed?'

'Where you going, Dan?'

'Out! I'm headin' for the plains, Betsy. I'm gonna make me a home where the buffalo roam.'

Later she'd throw plates into the sink with such venom they'd sometimes smash. She'd smoke a fag, have a long chew on the bottom lip, then get on the phone and give out yards to a sister. Later she'd roar at the child and her brow would crease up as she plotted an escape. Later she'd weep like a crone because she was lonely.

Dan'd be down the Dock Road, doing a string of bars and getting knee tremblers off fast girls in behind chip shop walls. Dan'd be going to dances out Drumkeen and swinging them around the floor, making husky promises beneath the candy-coloured lights. He'd sing 'Are The Stars Out Tonight?' as he walked them home. He'd play Russian hands and Roman fingers.

But the way it happens sometimes is that pain becomes a feed for courage, a nutrient for it: when pain drips steadily, it can embolden. She worked up the courage and left him, and left the young fella, too. It was a Halloween she went—Foley was dunking for apples. He was near enough reared, and he was the head off his father. She moved to Tipp town, or was it Nenagh, and fell in love with a book-maker there and died a happy woman. The lights went down on the Foley boys. They didn't get on. Violent confrontation was the daily norm and the worst of it, like in a country song, was when Foley started to win.

He hits the suburbs of the town and takes the Dock Road into the heart of the place. He steps away from the water and enters the grid of her streets, and his mood improves. He has before him the conso-lations of routine. He will go to the shade and dampness of the base-ment flat, where mushrooms have been known to grow from the walls. It is not much of a place to lay your head, no, but it is near the bar where they are used to him sitting in the shadows. (Lou Ferringo, they call him there, but not to his face.) It's near the place he buys the fish. It's where he braces himself for the afternoon walks by the creek, and we all have our creeks. He will put eight mackerel in two frying pans and fourteen potatoes in the big pot. He will turn on the television and go to page two-two-zero of the text to check on the football news. He will sigh then and stretch and take the keys of the car from the saucer by the door. At eight o'clock, precisely, he will turn the key in the ignition, put his size seventeen to the floor and he'll switch on the two-way radio.

'Fourteen here, base. I'm just heading out.'

And Alice at the base will say:

'Okay, Tom, can you pick up in Thomondgate for me? The

Gateway Bar. Sullivan.'

'Uh-oh. What kind of a way is he?'

'He doesn't sound great, Tommy.'

'I'll see what I can do.'

And for eight hours he'll pinball all over town—Thomondgate and Kileely, Prospect, Monaleen—and there is a sort of calmness in this and calmness accrues, it builds up like equity.

Maybe Foley will pick you up some night. You've had a few at The Gateway, or you've taken a hammering at the dogs, or you're stood in the rain with bags at your feet outside the Roxboro Tesco.

'Busy tonight?'

'Ah, we're kept going, you know? It's busy enough for a Monday.'

And you'll take him for an easeful man, a serene giant at the wheel of a gliding Nissan. Sometimes even the briefest touch is enough: you hand him the fare and he hands back the change and you feel the strange quiver, its coldness. He can tell precisely, in each case but his own. The town will lie flat and desolate and open to all weathers.

Ideal Homes

It was among the last bucolic fantasies of the village that Mr Delahunty, the blind shopkeeper, was secure against chancers and thieves. He could almost believe it himself, as cheerful villagers sang out the items they'd placed before him and his lively thin fingers danced across the register's keys. Mr Delahunty kept a mental ledger containing every last price in his shop and to locate a price, he simply rolled the eyes up into the top of his head. When they came down again, they were wet smears, unpleasantly viscous, like the albumen of half-boiled eggs, but they had the price got. Omo, the large, a woman would say, and the eyes of Delahunty would roll up quickly and as quickly return. Two forty-eight, he'd say, and rack it on the reg: the figures would roll.

This was as close as the village got to an attraction. The village was an unimpressive tangle of a dozen streets. There was a main street and a square, one as drab as the other, and a woeful few streets subsidiary to these. There was an insignificant river, brown and slow, and granite hills beyond—these, it was said, gave the place a scenic charm but in truth, it was forlorn. The people were terraced in neat rows and roofed in with grey slates and were themselves forlorn, but they wouldn't easily have said why.

Delahunty—his remaining senses sharpened—wasn't crazy about the way things were shaping up. Sometimes, on these quiet evenings, when the streets had emptied out, and the traffic had exhausted itself, and when the twins, Donna and Dee, moved swiftly through his aisles, the eyes of Delahunty rolled up not to search out a price but with suspicion and fear. The blind man could tell bad girls by smell.

'Just having a quick gawk, Mr Delahunty,' called Dee, the blonde, as she rifled the cooler for sugary drinks.

'Any sign at all of that new *Smash Hits*?' called Donna, the brunette, who daily skinned the magazine rack of its gaudier titles.

'No sign yet,' said Mr Delahunty. 'Anythin' else I'd do ye for?'

In her own good time, Donna sashayed from the aisles and slapped a single packet of mints onto the counter. Her stonewashed jeans were lumpy with swag. Dee, shipping in alongside, was already quietly taking the wrapper off a Lion Bar. They had neck and brass and tongues like lizards.

'Just these so,' said Donna. 'The auld bucks is tight.'

'What's it we have, ladies?'

'Polos,' said Dee. 'The mint with the hole in it.'

Mr Delahunty blushed to a purplish colour, like a winegum, and Donna didn't even pretend to hide her snigger.

'Breakin' hearts tonight, I suppose?' he tried to skip past the blush.

'Isn't much around this place you'd break 'em off,' said Donna. 'But we're causing damage all the same.'

'Trying the handles of parked cars,' said Dee.

'Whistling past the graveyard,' said Donna.

'Haven't they the lip taken off ye yet below in the Prez?' asked Delahunty.

'Sure you'd wonder what they're turning out of that school at all,' said Donna.

'Eejits,' said Dee. 'That place is nothin' only an eejit factory.'

'Ye'll be the stone cold end of me,' said Delahunty. 'That's twelve pence, please.'

Donna put the coins on the table and she let her fingers linger there to playfully tip against the blind man's reaching ones.

'See ya later, maybe?' she breathed it, heavily, and Dee made a wet, intimate noise with her painted lips.

Into the fade of a September evening, the two of them, brazen and sixteen. They were tallish in wedge heels. They were visions in stonewash. The hair was teased out big. There had been long hours of painful backcombing. The sky's weak glow was the glow of a mean coal fire tamped down with slack—a widower's fire. They made short work of the haul from Delahunty's and whirled into a sugar frenzy. Their chatter was so nervous as to edge on violence but it succumbed, after a few turns around the square, to the notes of cheap melody. They hummed an old waltz tune, like one from the fifties films their mother watched in the afternoons—valium and vodka, curtains drawn, big woozy romantic strings—and Donna hooked an arm of Dee's with a crook of her own, and they spun each other in slow then quickening circles, the footwork was dainty, the heels became a blur, down half the length of the main street they turned. There was a hooded crow on a windowsill. There was a notice for a sale of work pinned upside down in the display case by the grotto. All the parked cars pointed in the same direction.

They were dizzy and excited, wearing trouble as a scent, and they made for the next light that burned, which was the Yangtzee River, where they had a boyfriend installed: Lawrence Wang, its lone son and heir.

He was taking orders on the phone. He was feeding orders back to the wordless scowling father in the kitchen. He was keeping one eye trained on the small television ledged above the waiting area, which mutely showed the prices, the tote and the bursts of pelting action from a dog meeting. He watched it through the fag smoke of a Consulate wedged in the corner of his mouth. He kept the phone tucked beneath his chin.

'Chips or fried rice?' he said, and the door exploded, the bould ones burst in.

'What's cookin', Lala?' enquired Dee, putting bruised elbows and a swell of young chest on the counter before him.

'What's happenin', Babycakes?' enquired Donna, shipping in alongside.

'Half an hour,' Lawrence Wang told the phone.

He replaced the receiver. He stubbed out his cigarette. He lit his hardest glare.

'The two of ye can go park it somewhere else now, d'ye hear me?'

'Lala,' said Dee, 'would you do us a twirl there and give us a gander at them pert little buns?'

'I never seen a young fella fill a pair of Farahs like it,' said Donna, and she let her eyes turn in to meet one another.

Lawrence Wang glanced anxiously over his shoulder. He could rehearse the brush-off all he wanted but he could never bring it out when it was needed.

'Swear to God,' he whispered, 'if he catches ye in here again! This is the busy time and I wouldn't mind but ye were told.'

'Busy alright,' said Dee, swivelling her gaze around the empty take-away.

'Dancing room only at the Yangtzee River,' said Donna, and she waltzed herself to the far wall, where the menu was pinned.

Lawrence looked past them. He gazed with great adolescent suffering into the cold eight o'clock street, to the dwindling terraces across the way, the voodoo hills beyond. The village so quickly ran out of itself: it turned into rough ground, rose to the hills and dark sky. The ground was taking wounds up there. He didn't need to see Donna and Dee this evening. He had notions himself and they'd only give a charge and impetus to them. He had great self-awareness for a young fella. He knew full well that he was after falling in with a bad crowd—sometimes two is plenty enough to be a crowd.

'Are ye orderin' something now or are ye coolin' heels?' he said.

Dee raised the back of her hand to her forehead, fluttered her lids and performed an MGM swoon.

'Lawrence,' she said. 'There's a tremendous coldness about you tonight, darling.'

Donna clutched violently at her abdomen, as though shot, and she slithered down the far wall.

'Oh!' she cried. 'Oh what a sublime corpse!'

'Jesus, can't ye keep quiet? He'll be out!'

But it was already too late. The swing door from the kitchen creaked an entrance: Mr Wang appeared. He hissed a string of dangerous Cantonese at his son, who nodded apology and compliance.

'Howya this weather, Mr Wang?' called Dee. 'Shockin' draw in the evenings.'

'Why she on floor?' Mr Wang furiously observed her sister.

'I'm shot, Johnny! I'm all shot up!' cried Donna.

'I'd chance the sweet 'n' sour,' said Dee, 'if the chicken had wings.'

'If the chicken wasn't 16-to-1 at Shelbourne Park,' said Donna.

Such cheek was beyond Mr Wang. He could but glare at them and, more meaningfully, at his son. There would be hysterical words later on, inside by the flypaper and the heat of the fryers. He withdrew.

'Leg it!' said Lawrence. 'Lively!'

'You know what'd shift us?' said Donna. 'Toss out the keys of the motor there, would ya?'

Lawrence Wang drove a silvery sports car. Often, on the summer nights, the twins had shared the passenger seat and by long assault on his patience, and by promise of favours to come, they had cajoled him into allowing turns at the wheel. Fast rounds of the industrial estate were performed—they by principle refused to slow down for ramps. One night, with Lawrence Wang reduced to tears, and with Dee on his lap, Donna had driven clear of the estate and onto the dual carriageway, where she performed a near-flawless handbrake turn.

'Git!' said Lawrence Wang.

'Go on, La, one lap of Mondello.'

'Out! Now!'

Among the fantasies of the village already fallen was that its terrace doors might be left unlocked. That one hadn't survived the night poor Annie Quinlan came down to her kitchen for a sup of water only to find a hardchaw from Ennis on the floor in front of her, with a tyre iron in his hand. The village by quiet consent then entered the age of security, and its citizens were particularly pleased with their dead bolts, their strobe alarms and their attack dogs when they twitched the curtains of an evening and saw Donna and Dee approaching, with that evil, vivacious, whistling air.

'Don't gimme no back talk, sucka!' Donna roared at the Marian statue in the square, for the twins were reverent devotees of The A-Team.

They aimed toes for Pa Hurley's garage. It was in the west end, and you'd tell it quick enough because the man himself had painted in red block letters on its gable wall the legend:

PA HURLEY'S GARAGE.

Pa kept late hours. Pa hadn't much choice in the matter. People wanted their cars back to them quick. All the patience was gone out of people, and sure enough, the twins found him on the premises. He was involved with the nether regions of a mint-green Cortina.

'Howya, Pa?' they sang, in a tone that might turn a lesser man to religion, but Pa Hurley was fond of himself and on a good night would think he had the measure of them. Suavely, he slid from beneath the motor, raised himself onto an elbow, regarded them slowly, grazed his eyes from north pole to south, and smirked.

'How ye keepin' yereselves?'

'Ah,' said Donna, letting sad eyes drift to the hills, 'there's nights you'd find yourself with a strange auld longin'.'

Dee picked up a phase tester and twirled it, slowly, then laid its cool steel against her cheek.

'I've a class of a want meself,' she said. 'But I couldn't put a finger on it.'

Donna planted herself on the bonnet of a tan Beetle, crossed her legs at the ankles and assumed a Miss Ireland glaze. Dee put the full five ten of herself at a haughty stand in front of Pa Hurley: it was a pose learned from a Joan Jett video, with the heels planted wide and the perky nose in the air. The phase tester was now threateningly gripped.

'Time you knockin' off, Bub?' she said

Pa Hurley rose. He laughed softly. He took some of the oil off his hands with a rag. He looked around him for fear of neighbours. He was forty and drearily married. Each morning, in the bleakest of hours—the one that comes before first light—he woke to a desperate lust for his own youth. It came in bits of old songs and lines from old films and in the remembered music of old girlfriends' voices. He could never shake these twinges, not even if he put the pillow over

his head against them. The twins had caught this yearning in him—
something similar had made a moon-gazer of their own poor
father—and they played on it.

'Now listen up, Randy, and listen good,' said Donna. 'What say
we steal a car and break for the border?'

''Ve vill make Mexico by dawn,' said Dee.

'We will,' said Pa Hurley. 'How're things with ye anyway?'

Always, as soon as he was properly exposed to the twins' presence, to the hum of their animal vitality, the cheek went out of him.
This effect on men wasn't unusual in their short experience.

'Couldn't be better, Pa,' said Dee. 'The hay is in and Cork are
bate and all the beans are comin' up in their lovely little rows.'

'How're things with ye really?' he said, and there was a hint of
anger, he didn't know where it came from or why.

'How's herself above, Pa?' said Donna, delighted at the spit in
him. 'Is she looking after you good?'

'She's holding fairly well, Pa, in all fairness like,' said Dee. 'That
was any amount of a coat she'd on her Saturday night.'

'Go handy now,' he said and he looked to the ground—their lipstick and their lip gloss sealed his fate.

'You're treatin' her right anyway,' said Donna. 'God knows don't
she deserve it.'

'No woman deserves it more,' said Dee.

'Fond of it, I'd say,' said Donna.

'Like her mother before her,' said Dee.

Pa Hurley tried to warn them off with a dangerous look but it
was only encouragement.

'Did ye knock out to the new bar Saturday, Pa?'

'We did, yeah.'

'No expense spared. Heard the Guinness there is brutal altogether?'

'Not a great pint,' he agreed.

'Heard it was like disco Guinness. Would we get in, would you say?'

'Not a chance,' said Pa Hurley. 'It's a respectable establishment.'

'Back in the knife drawer, ducky,' said Donna.

'Chance at all you'd give us a lift, Pa?' asked Dee.

'A lift where?' he said.

He was wary. He would flirt if he had the mood or drink on him but Pa Hurley was beat if an actual plan was broached.

'Ah sure,' said Donna, 'wherever. We could go watch a film or something.'

'Ye're lethal,' he said. 'There's poor young fellas will do jail for ye.'

'Who owns the Beetle, Pa?'

'Forget about it!'

'Half an hour, Pa. There won't be a single mark on it.'

'Never again!' he said. 'Look, d'ye want a few fags?'

They cleaned him out of Bensons. They peeled him with sneers. They hissed over their shoulders that he was nothing only a grease monkey but sure they'd call again anyway, all the best, Pa, keep in by the wall.

They went back among the streets. They sniffed disdainfully as they passed the gates of the Prez, from which they were serving another suspension. They stopped by the window of Daly the butcher. Daly had skinned rabbits hanging there; the display was lit by a pink sacred heart bulb. Though empty for the night, the spirit of Daly filled his shop yet: a whiskey-nosed presence, with the mad cleaver swinging. A fantasy of the village maintained by Daly was that its people were hearty, hill country eaters, as they had been in the days of his father's butchering. He shot and skinned the rabbits himself and hung them for weeks until they were all but maggoty. Forlornly, then, they'd be brought home to feed the family of Dalys, who had rabbit coming out their ears. The cruel fact was that all Daly ever managed to sell these days was chicken nuggets. The twins were mesmerised by the skinned rabbits. The wine-coloured flesh, with maplines of blue for the hardened veins, and the taut muscles and tendons that still gave a sense of momentum, of swiftness perfected: the hung and skinned rabbits were frozen speed. This was the one moment of the day the twins were without front. There was dark wonder in them.

'I pity the fool!' said Donna, breaking the spell.

'First name: Mista. Middle name: Period. Last name: T,' said Dee.

Out the other end of the village they swung, to where the new estate was being built. The wire rails erected to secure the site had been left unchained. They squeezed through. They walked the raw crescents of the brownfield site in the thickening dark. A uniform shape was emerging. There were glassless windows and slateless roofs. Trenches were being cleared for sewage. The site was on the first steep rise of the hills and it was assaulted at all times by wind: the people who'd come to live here would be skinned themselves. There was a view south to the city: it was ever spreading, quick approaching. It was ten miles wide of sodium light, a sea of promise laid out beneath them. They drank it in and tasted faster nights to come.

They found a JCB left unlocked. They climbed up it. With the slap of a wedge heel Dee broke off the panel and the wires dangled. They'd an idea which ones to manipulate and to their great delight, the JCB growled to life.

'Gonna open us a can o' whupass,' said Donna.

The JCB was steered past the eerie new houses and given some juice to batter aside the wire rails. They hummed soft love songs as they went, they smoked Bensons. They emerged to the village streets. They were not expected anywhere, not anytime soon. The accelerator was floored. They had proper road under them now.

'Let's see what this baby can do,' said Dee.

The change that had come was mostly unseen. It took place behind closed doors, in front rooms and back kitchens, in bedrooms, in the heart. But if it was unseen, it was not unheard. Mr Delahunty, as he pulled the shutters and felt for the padlock, oh Delahunty could hear it well enough. It was a gear change, a low rumbling, a faint groaning beneath the skin of the earth. The ground was readying itself for new life.

The Wintersongs

The train pulled into a country station and they piled on board with country groans and country winces. There was hard wheezing and there were low whistles of dismay, as though they were half crucified from the effort of it all. They carried raw November on the breath. They carried phones, food, magazines. They eyeballed seats and shuffled towards the seats, they asked were the seats taken, for form's sake, but they didn't wait for an answer—it would take shotguns to keep them out of the seats. The girl tried to project belligerence or even menace but the old woman sat opposite just the same. She was bony and long and turkey-necked, ancient but with a fluency in the features, a face where age surfaces and then recedes again. She wasn't at all shy.

Good morning, miss, she said. And I'll beg your pardon, because the sweat is drippin' off me. It was touch and go whether I'd make it at all. We have tar taken off that road coming up from the quare place. I'm after getting a lift off the younger one of the Canavans. The small fella, with the arm. Of course you might as well get a lift off a stone but I suppose the Canavans were always odd. He sitting there, bulling, you'd think he was after donating an organ to me. But anyway, I'm here, and I'm in the one piece, just about. What have we? Nine o'clock. Nine, and I've half a day put down. What did you say your name was? Lovely. And is that with an 'h'?

A slow rumbling, then the sullen build of momentum, and the countryside was unpeeled, image by image: an old house with its slate roof caved in; magpies bossing a field; on higher ground, a twist of grey trees in the grudging light. The girl made a broad mime of adjusting her iPod, and she assumed a dead-eyed glaze, but the old woman smiled, shuffled to rearrange her bony buttocks for comfort, entwined her thin fingers and clasped them about her middle, then rotated one thumb slowly around the other.

Would you believe, she said, that I was up for half six? Sitting in the kitchen in front of a two-bar fire, with the jaws hanging open. You see I didn't want to miss Canavan. And it's not as if I had sleep to distract me. Sure there's no more such thing as sleep. Do you know the way? Of course you don't. What age did you say you were? Hah! So you were born—I'll do the maths—you were born in 19… 88? My God. The Seoul Olympics. What was his name, with the big eyes? Ben Johnson. Only a mother could love it. Of course I lost a kidney in 1988. But yes, four o'clock in the morning, and I'm staring at the ceiling… when it's springtime in Australia, it's Christmas over here. Did you ever hear that one? No, well, it's before your time I suppose. Here, above, watch—new road. This is the by-pass they're after putting down. Look. Look! They're going to cut out Nenagh altogether. No harm.

If there was a heat-seeking device high up, mapping all movement by the glow of the blood, it would pick them out as two pulsing red ovals—tiny dots on a vast map. They moved eastwards at ninety rickety miles an hour and the old woman leaned across as though to confide and the ovals conjoined and pulsed almost as one. The girl took out a book and made a display of it. She peeled a clementine and looked to the passing skies. She tried to put a fence up, but the old one was a talker.

What if I told you, she said, that I can see how it'll work out? What if I said it's written all over your face? Pay no attention. I'm rambling. I'm only fooling with you. You'd think someone would come along and throw a shovel of earth over me. So would you head up often yourself? I go regular. Not that I'd have a great deal of business but I have the pass. Shoes, occasionally. I pick up shoes for a woman in Birdhill. There's a shop above that specialises in extreme sizes. She's a fourteen. I know, but we have to try not to be cruel in life. That's the most important thing. And it's an excellent shop. They'll do you a practical boot, or a runner, or something dressy. Or as dressy as you're going to get if you're a fourteen. Don't! This is a poor woman, the first thing she thinks about of a morning is feet. You step out of the bed and there they are. Always and forever, clomping along beneath you, like boats. You run for a bus. You step onto a dance floor. You try to pull on a pair of nylons. I'm a three myself—look. A three. Dainty.

Through and on, North Tipperary, weary hedgerows, and chimney pots, and the far-out satellite towns of reason, all of it stunned looking with the onslaught of winter, as if winter was a surprise to the place, and there were frequent apparitions—heavy-set men rolling tyres and twirling wrenches, stepping down from lorries, giving out to phones—and it darkened, as though on a dimmer switch, the morning became smudged and inky.

Losing the wheels, she said, was rough. When you've no wheels, the options are limited. You'd be inclined to pack it in altogether. Of course if I had sense, I'd be driving still but I rode my luck and it gave out. I turned it over outside Tullamore. They'd every right to take the course of action they took. The startling thing was there wasn't a mark on me and the car a write-off. They threw the book at me and they had every justification. It was eight in the evening, for God's sake, it was summer, it was still daylight, and I'm on the Tullamore Road after making shit out of a Fiesta? I ask you. I defended myself. I said, your honour, please don't take this event in isolation. I went back forty years. I told him how it all turned crooked on me. How you can't run away from things, you only store them for later. I gave him chapter and verse. Not that I thought I was going to walk out with a licence in my hand. I just wanted to explain. I just wanted to say. Of course, the eyes rolled up in his head. As a matter of fact, your honour, I said, I have no intention of ever driving again. And he looks down at me, over the top of the glasses, and he says, Madam, I am here to facilitate your wishes. Lovely deep voice on him. A gentleman.

The haggard verges of a town put in an appearance. Motor factors, light industry, ribbon development, new-build schemes, the health centre, an Aldi. Here was sweet life, and the common run, also the shades of mild hysteria. Here was...

Templemore, she said. I can never pass through without thinking of poor Edward. My cousin. The misfortune, you see this is where they train guards, and he was mad to get in. It's not the case now. I understand there's a shortage. But Edward was... you could only say... OBSESSED! He nearly went out of his mind. You had to be five ten in your stockinged feet and he was five nine and a half. Just that fraction shy and it sent the poor creature to his wit's end. All he wanted in life was to be a guard. I have nothing against guards myself, despite what happened to me in Thurles. Of course that was my own fault as well. But Edward? A half inch. And what happened? His father, my uncle, Joe, God rest him, a very intelligent man, though lazy, Joe got up out of the chair and he got two sheets. With one of them he bound his son at the wrists and with the other he bound him at the ankles. He tied one end to the bumper of the car and he tied the other to the back axle of the tractor. I think it was a Belarussian they had. A powerful machine. And he climbed onto it and he looked out back and he called down, Edward! EDWARD!

Heads swivelled in the carriage. Newspapers were raised just a little bit higher. They said it with their eyes—we have one across the way, watch? Careful now.

Edward, he said, son, there's no pressure on you. And Edward looked up at him and he said, Da? Start that engine. That same day Edward strode back into Templemore. He took off the shoes and he stood up against the wall and he said MEASURE ME! And he wasn't five foot ten. He was five eleven. If you want to talk about dedication. If you want to talk about a man with hope. He would always say after it was an extraordinary length to go to. That's as true as I'm sitting here, Sarah, even if the guards didn't work out great for him in the end. And by the way, would you mind taking that thing out of your ears while I'm talking to you?

The light was scratched, molecular, the sky about to give in on itself, about to break up, a mist descending already, and they went slowly through and on, at a creaking rumble, then it built up on a straight stretch, and there was a descent to the midland plain, where confused-looking ducks sailed a small drowsy lake. The trolley went past—flattened vowels, lazy wheels, scalding drinks—teascoffees, lads, ladies? Teascoffees? By a tiny grey village there stood an enormous pink funeral home.

Death, she said. Would you think about death much, Sarah? Of course you wouldn't. I dare say you have other things on your mind. I've been meaning to ask, actually, have we a boyfriend on the scene? No? Come off it! Who are you trying to kid? I'd say they're like flies around you. I'd say they can barely keep a hold of themselves. No? Well I suppose you could do with weight. Excuse me, what muffins have you? I see. I'll chance a blueberry.

They outpaced the weather, by and by, and the arcs of a weak sun swung across the waiting fields, and the country eased into itself, and there was woodland passing. The girl considered changing seats but she didn't want to be rude. Some days you suffer.

Trees, said the old woman. What's it they call it? Photosynthesis. Amazing what you'd remember, for years. Is it chloroform or chlorophyll? Or is that toothpaste? Or is it tap water? Or is it what the dentist put on rags? I'm dating myself. Trees! Calming, apparently. Or so they'd tell you. I wouldn't be too sure. Would you believe it if I told you I was walking through a wood one day—this is in Clare I'm talking about—and I saw a man buried to the neck? Only a young fella. This time of the year. It would have been mulchy underfoot. Whatever way he managed it, he scratched out a hole in the ground and dragged the earth in after him. Buried to the neck. Some job of work. Now the young fella wasn't *well*, obviously. It turned out after he was known around the place. It wasn't his first time at this kind of messing. Of course it was just my luck to come across him. Who else would go out for a breath of air and walk into the likes of it? And what are you supposed to say to someone? You'd want nerves of steel to deal with that kind of situation and do I look as if I have nerves of steel? Trees! Arbour. Isn't it? *Arboreal*. There's a word for you. Lovely. Photosynthesise. Come on we all go and photosynthesise. Trees can give you a sore throat. Something in the sap I think. Put me near trees and I find the throat goes septic on me. I come over class of hoarse. I come over husky. On account of trees. Septic. Sceptic. Anyway, tell me, Sarah, what's it you're reading? Go 'way? And would you be much of a one for the reading?

Her face seemed to slip, her features came loose, disintegrated, and then rearranged. She was slippery. She was skinny, tall, sharp angled and grey skinned, with ash-coloured eyes and green-mottled hands, and now it was a pretty, blowy day, with screensaver skies. They made it to the flats and paddocks of the Curragh, a watery expanse it seemed, a lightly-ruffled sea.

Horses, she said. Sweet Jesus don't be talking to me about horses. The worst thing that can happen with horses happened me. The first time I set foot on a racecourse, I went through the card. Limerick meeting—there were seven races, I picked seven winners. The whole cruel world of work and bosses and punching clocks at seven in the morning was revealed to me as a sham, Sarah, a world for fools. Who needed it? All you had to do was have a go at the horses.

She wiped muffin crumbs from her chin. She lifted her rueful heavy eyes to the heavens. She smiled.

Of course I wasn't the first eejit to come up with this idea. It took no more than six months and I was wiped out. I found myself in desperate waters. The bank pulled the shutters when it saw me coming. My name was doing the rounds in faxes, twice underlined. I was blacklisted by every credit union in South Tipp, North Waterford, East Cork. But there's always someone you can turn to and they showed up, soon enough. Two brothers, from Thurles, serious operators, hair and eyebrows, big shoulders. These boys were beef to the heels. If I'd sense, I'd have run a mile but do I look as if I have sense? I missed a payment and they showed up for a polite word. I missed a second payment and I was backed into the corner of a lounge bar. Oh, a monster! Did you realise, Sarah, that monsters are all around us? You've come to the right woman. I missed a third payment and that was it, I had to clear out of Tipp altogether. If I didn't get out, it was looking like a boot-of-the-car job. I drove off late. Night-time, cold, and there were dogs somewhere, howling. I rang the boys from a payphone, I couldn't resist. I said d'ye call yereselves men? To threaten a poor single woman? Spittin' feathers down the phone he was. I'd have to be careful to this day about setting foot in Thurles. But that's no great loss to me. Of course the nerves weren't right for a long while. I was edgy, Sarah. I was drinking against nerves. It wasn't long after I lost most of the teeth. I missed a step on an embankment. Would you believe it if I told you these are nearly all screw-ins? They're some job, aren't they? Thank you. Of course I paid for them in tears. I was six months on soup and custard. And if the horses were bad, you should have seen me the year of the poker machines. I still get a shake in my right hand when I hear one.

They were by the last stretch of countryside, above the surging drag of the motorway, and the exurbs crept out west, and a squat grey building sat high on a windy rise, and she pointed, and winked.

Do you see this place? she said. Do you know what that used to be? Chained to the walls, Sarah. Which end is the sleeves? Are we coming or going? Here's one you'll not have heard, I guarantee it. Nachtmusik! Have you ever hear that word? It's a good one, isn't it? Out of the Germans, and faith they'd know all about it. Going loco down in Acupulco. The soft room. The slow-shoed shuffle in the corridor. The hair stood up on your head from shocks. If the walls could talk in the likes of that place! El Casa des Locos is what a Spaniard would say. They've apartments made of it now. Best of luck to them all inside.

She simmered with happiness. There was great calm about her. There was no reserve about her. There was none of the wistfulness proper to old age. It was clammy on the train, and she opened her coat and loosened the collar of her blouse, and there was a cheap chain and cross on her neck—it flashed with trinket menace. For a while, she was silent, and the silence was unbearable. Her gaze went to the carriage roof, all to be seen were the whites of her eyes. She hummed to herself, crossed over, then returned.

What about yourself? she said. I wouldn't go so far as to call you the chatty type. What's your own situation? Do you want me to take a run at it?

She rubbed her hands: lascivious. She made as though to sketch in the air. She took on a high-toned expression. She drew broad strokes with bony fingers. She cupped her chin in her palms.

Let's see what we've got, she said. The eyes are outside your head, so you were up at a dirty hour yourself. You got dressed in the dark, didn't you? Yes, with a big brazen head, very sure of yourself. The case was packed since last night, you did it on the sly. You had it hid under the stairs. You went down the stairs and got the case and you opened the front door, very quiet, and you stepped out into the street. It's a terrace of houses, isn't it? Familiar as your own face but unreal at that hour: parked cars, frost, moon, not a cat on the road. You pulled the door out after you. You could hardly breathe.

And the light was starting to come through then. She went down the steps by the grotto. She went down into the bowl of the town. There was yeast in the air from the brewery. Some early workers were eating eggs in the café on the corner, lost in newspapers, winter, the steam of their tea. She went inside to get cigarettes from the machine and the men looked up, and they looked at each other. There were affectations of great sadness—a pretty girl in a pencil skirt can bring that on easy enough. A dozy smile from the plump familiar waitress, but nobody asked any questions, nobody asked where are you going so early, Sarah, and what's with the case, girl? She went down McCurtain Street and she watched herself as she went, she painted in the drama of it. She bought a ticket at Kent Station. A single: she stressed the word. She sat on a high stool and sipped coffee and a tic of anxiety surfaced, a bird-like flutter beneath the skin. The man from the kiosk was on his knees cutting a bale of newspapers with a penknife and its blade was a blue gleam.

You'd be mistaken for angelic, said the old woman. Peachy-creamy, oh lovely, look—petite! But there's awful distance in you.

She smiled but it was sardonic, ironical.

There's coldness, isn't there, Sarah? You were going to get out as soon as you could and not a word to anyone about it. To hell with it—let 'em suffer!

The world around withdrew from them. The woman reached across the table and took the girl's slate-cold hands in hers. The pulsing ovals weakened, faded, and disappeared. There was no sound except for a soft, lone breathing. There was no way to reverse from this, or to pull back.

Listen, she said. I have news for you. Brace yourself, child, 'cause here it comes. There is no such thing as forgiveness. Everything has a consequence. Would you believe that? Years later, you'll still have to answer the question: was the right thing done?

The girl looked away, abruptly, into the steel glimmer of the morning. She bit on her bottom lip, so prettily. It would be hopeless to try and find a flaw on her.

I wouldn't fret about it, said the old woman. Maybe it was the right thing. He didn't have the courage, did he? He wouldn't say how he felt. He wouldn't tell you how he felt, Sarah. You see you have to stand up for it. You have to declare it.

Then it was the Clondalkin yards, mostly disused, and the dust and seep of the city had fallen on them. The train stopped to take on maintenance workers. Another train was stalled alongside, it was headed in the opposite direction. Passengers from each stared wearily across to the other. Movement, and she felt as though her train had eased slowly forwards but it was the other, pulling away west. The old woman went out through the yards. She threw no shadow in the white sun. She went over the sidings and past the rusted trailers. She went in among the carriage-building sheds and vanished, left no trace. She became light, air, dust.

Now it's Heuston and here she comes. A thin girl in a pencil skirt, pulling a trolley-case behind, and the midday crush parts before her like a miraculous sea. She flips the key-guard of her phone and scrolls her texts. She moves on again, straight-backed and hard-eyed, with world-class invulnerability. She doesn't know that every step from now will change her. She is so open, so fluid. Every conversation will change her, every chance meeting, every walk down the street. Every walk; every street.

Party At Helen's

How does a young fella born to a place of dismal fields and cold stone churches turn out to be fuck-off cool? How do you compute boreens and crows and dishwater skies and make it add up to a nineteen year old who walks into a party and every girl in the place goes loop-the-loop?

But not walks—walked. The party has been over for fifteen years. It was in Galway, a Saturday night, a Sunday morning, after the nightclubs had closed and the late roar of the streets had started to break up. A couple of dozen people—you'd say children, if you could see them now—went back, in pairs and in small groups, to a rented house. Most of them were still mashed on cheap nightclub drugs. The house had tongue-and-groove walls greening with damp and was filled with the smell of the damp and with the cloying waft of a low-grade cannabis resin. It was a little past four. The panes of the sash windows trembled with vibration from the music that was playing and the miserable furniture was pushed back to the walls. He went alone to a vantage corner. He hunched down on his heels and scoped out the ground. The girls wore lycra and had their hair styled in blunt retro fringes, like Jane Fonda in Barbarella. They wore clumpy shoes and tiny silver dresses, or flight jackets with heavy fur collars, they wore Lacoste, Fila and Le Coq Sportif. He sized them up, one by one, from ankles to nape, and he paid special attention to the tendons and the neck muscles; he was a canny young farmer at mart.

He made his decision, quickly and without fuss. He crossed the room towards where she was dancing and he said hi. She ignored him. He felt dry-mouthed, tense with concentration, excited. He would need to follow her eyes, carefully, and find the words that would lighten them. This was work. She was aloof and this had its magneticism and he may have begun to despair but he received a quick enquiring glance from over her shoulder and so was heartened. Gesture politics, in an old house, on a rough winter's night, down a backstreet of Galway. There was water moving nearby, it wasn't far from the Claddagh. She had a hindquarter on her it was unbelievable.

'I saw you at Wiped, yeah?'

'Yeah?'

'Yeah. What was your name again?'

'Martina.'

Two words were enough to give it away as a Clare accent, flat and somehow accusatory, an accent he didn't approve of, normally, but she was good-looking enough to get away with it. His accent was from further north, and a shade east, pure Roscommon. It was designed for roaring over chainsaws and horsing out ballads to the fallen martyrs of Irish republicanism but he had honed it, somehow, to a hoarse-sounding, late-night cool.

Around them, all was nervousness and elation. Lit up like stars, everybody loved everybody, and there was little shyness about saying so. Hugs and love and tearful embraces. It was all tremendously fluffy. These were children born to unions of a pragmatism so dry it chaffed, they came from supper tables livid with silence, they came down from marriages where the L-word hadn't darkened the door in decades. There was the feeling of sweat from the nightclub cooling on the small of your back.

He wore a number two cut, it was Daxed and brushed forward, and the sideburns were daily tended to. He by habit checked out people's shoes: she was wearing Fila creepers, of which he approved. He owned three hundred and eighty-seven twelve-inch records, mostly made in Berlin, Sheffield or Detroit. He had a father with a head like a boiled ham.

'It's coming on in waves, like.'

'Yeah,' she said, 'I know what you mean.'

Not by any stretch of the imagination could you say she had big tits but fine, really, at least not like your one out of the art college the other week, like an ironing board she was.

'Waves,' he said, and he chewed his jaws and rolled his shoulders.

The windows shuddered with bass and rattled with wind. There were the usual January gales off the Bay. It was one of those nights you'd be skinned walking down Spanish Arch, if you were heading for the taxis on Dominick Street. He weighed up his chances of getting her into a taxi and out the far end of Salthill. He lived in a bedsit there the size of a shoebox. He could make tea and toast without getting out of the bed. It was a row of old seaside boarding houses, mostly in disrepair. He could see down to the prom, to the low breaking waters and the power walkers in rain gear, their garish colours moving quickly through the rain. He sometimes followed random women on the prom. Yummy-mummies, coming out of Mass or the Centra: he walked at a reasonable distance behind, and was pleasantly hypnotised by the swaying quick switches of their rears. He almost always managed to control himself but sometimes they were very pale and beautiful. He scribbled down their car regs, just to mark the sighting, for no other purpose than that. He kept a list of regs and descriptions in a folder beneath his bed.

Only once had he become fevered. That was the day he followed the woman to her house on Taylor's Hill. He had hauled up over the high wall and huddled in the wet garden behind her hedge. He peered into the kitchen—the light was on at three o'clock, it was such a dark afternoon—and he watched her boil a kettle for tea, the steam rising out of it, and the blood rushing in his ears. This was the most erotically-charged moment of October. He was on ketamine at the time.

'Waves, like,' he said. 'I think I'm coming up on the third one now. I wouldn't be surprised.'

She sensed something about him. When he looked at you, handsome and sharp-featured though he was, you got the feeling that comes after you've chewed a mouthful and you just know that the chicken is dodgy. She moved away from him. She went to her friend,

Alice. She asked Alice if she knew him.

'To see,' said Alice. 'Majorly cute. You must have seen him around the place. At Wiped and that. At Sex Kitchen?'

'Yeah but why is he always on his own though?'

'Maybe he's just a bit quiet,' said Alice.

Alice had a forgiving nature, especially when it came to men. She could find a good word to say about most anything in pants. She came from Tipperary and was the shape and texture of a kiwi fruit. She was so button-nosed you would think to press on it and hear a bell. She stood a jaunty five-nothing in her tallest heels. She was vivid, emotionally, and would make an opera out of the smallest crisis. She feared the routine and the humdrum. She sensed how easily these might overwhelm the paltry glamour available to a small wet college town in the west of Ireland. She was intuitive: she had an idea of the vast adult dullness that loomed around the next turn. She shook her head to be rid of the thought; tonight, she was hellbent on fun.

She drifted away from Martina, politely, still smiling. She loved her friend dearly but Martina was five ten and supple as a fawn: in the foreground perspective of a house party, the contrast-gain would not be Alice's. She went to the kitchen, where there was a congregation too sophisticated to dance, or too smashed, or too shy. Alice's gift was to immediately offer herself as an intimate and to be accepted as such. People let it all hang out when they talked to Alice. She enjoyed this but it could be a burden, too. She was left with little space for her own worries. Even her father had spilled to her, always, even when she was a kid, and with shit she didn't need to hear. This had made her mother jealous, even though she couldn't understand why. Theirs was the first divorce in Tipp after divorce came in.

Alice in the kitchen sat by Mary Pearson, and took her by the arm, and they listened, with glazed smiles, as Obran rattled on and on at one of his endless, self-aggrandising yarns. Mary kissed Alice's button nose and laid her long, elegant fingers across Alice's nervous knees. The manner of this, the languid ease of it, edged just a shade beyond chumminess. Mary Pearson had deep sexual talent and was becoming ever more comfortable in its realm. She was a slender, fine-boned twenty, plain-featured but attractive, with that particular charge of attractiveness that comes in freckles and neat chin and dirty eyes, and she applied it through the touch of her fingertips and Alice moved on again, bashful now. The kitchen stank of Wednesday's bolognese and drying sweat.

Mary listened to Obran ramble on—bollocks talk—and she watched Alice join another small huddle, and she watched the stunned, wordless lads from Connemara who had eaten too much ecstasy, and she smiled for Jack and Kay. She watched over them all with the fondness that is usually reserved for watching over small children. She was born to middle age, and a lascivious one: all solace was in the senses. She'd slept already with three of the boys and two of the girls at the party. She'd been notching them off in History and Politics, and she was working her way through the hockey union too. Her father owned half Ballinasloe. She had not talked to him since the horse fair, when he'd accused her of sleeping with an itinerant. She bored of Obran—anyway she'd already been—and she crossed the kitchen towards Jack and Kay, she was convinced she could talk them into it yet. Ollie stumbled as she passed and almost knocked her over.

'Ollie! For fucksake. Watch where you're going.'

'Lady Muck,' said Ollie, bowing. 'My sincere apologies, like.'

Ollie moved on through the hallway. He paused to steady himself with a hand on the hall table. The table had flyers for pizza, taxis and Jesus. That snot-nosed bitch, the look she always gave him. He peeped into the main room and it was writhing now—there had been a fresh intake from a party in Salthill broken up by guards. He decided that he had no interest at all in the main room. His business was done for the evening and anyway he felt short-breathed and tense and his vision was definitely blurred, especially out of the left eye. He went upstairs instead. He wore his puffa jacket, as he did at all times. He stuck his beany, bristled head into a small boxroom, saw that it was empty, and gratefully threw himself down on its lonesome single bed. Ollie had overdone it, again. Ollie had been overdoing it, in one or another, since he was big enough for shoes.

His eyes were frightened and atrocious, pissholes in the snow, and they gave him a comically tormented look, always, even if he was in good form. He was local. He sold amphetamine cut with paracetamol to students, and he signed on at three post offices, one in the city and two in the county. He drove a Corolla that was rotten with rust, it had neither tax nor insurance. He smoked too much cannabis. He drank like it was going out of style. He no longer had parents, he had six brothers who between them had six wives, nineteen children and twenty-eight dogs. His brothers would slag him about the seventh bride but Ollie had no interest in women, nor in men for that matter—he had interest in money, cannabis, cars, amphetamines and long-neck bottles of Corona lager. He had a kind of antic court jauntiness, almost medieval-seeming. There was no violence in him. There was vast bitterness in him. He made up stories out of the wet salty air, about people and for people, to frighten them and to entertain. He was currently putting it about that Mary Pearson had HIV. He was subject to magical thinking about the significance of the number nine. He put together a fat cone that used up five Rizlas and two entire Rothmans. He sucked down the lovely resins and immediately took on the notion that there were guards outside the house. They could have followed the crowd that came in from Salthill. Of course they could have. It wasn't just likely it was probable. He took another drag and felt his crown tighten and he decided it was certain, he didn't have a minute to spare. He went to the window and looked down to the parked cars, and to the shadows, and the rain blown across the town. There were plainclothes out there, of course there were, and they were waiting for him to make his move. Well, they hadn't bested him yet and they wouldn't tonight. It was Ollie's belief that he was tailed by plainclothes five or six days out of the week and he wasn't entirely mistaken in this. The window was an attic window—a cheap velour job set into the slate roof—and he saw that if he took off the puffa it would be easy enough to wriggle outside; he was slim-hipped as a ferret, and he could move along the rooftops of the terrace that the house was set on. Puffa out the window, and he climbed after it, with the cone wedged efficiently in the corner of his mouth, a dull burn. From the rooftop you could see to the cathedral, its wet concrete looming through the foul weather, and distant, the blur of the taxi-lights in rain, and all around the sodium gloom of the lamps. Ollie zipped into the puffa again and patted himself down to check for wallet, keys, lighter, fags, dope. He pressed back against the dripping slates and worked out his escape. He counted the chimneys along the length of the terrace—nine. He would need to climb to the other side, over the crease of the rooftop, and from there he could shin down a drainpipe into a yard, and then make his way down back towards the docks. So long as there were no dogs he'd be fine. He set to.

'Who'd leave a window open on a night like this? It's a fucking icebox in here.'

'Actually the breeze is kind of nice now, leave it open a while. Whose room is it anyway?'

'Probably Alan's. It certainly smells like a wankpit.'

'Does, doesn't it?'

'Well, if it's Alan we're talking about, there'll be no shortage of action,' and he made the jerk-off motion with his hand.

'Please, Jack. Not an image I want to stick. He's not here, is he?'

'Think he's home still. There are cows to be milked in Leitrim. There's no such thing as Christmas for cows, you know. Come here.'

'Fuck off.'

'What?'

'What what? Do you honestly believe I might be feeling romantic?'

'You're making too much out of this.'

'Easy for you to say.'

'I thought the plan was we weren't going to talk about it. Tuesday it's done with and we can forget about it.'

'It was crazy taking a pill.'

'What difference does it make, Kay? You're getting it looked after on Tuesday.'

'Looked after! This is starting to sound like something from the 1950s.'

'I know, yeah. She takes the lonesome boat. I am in the moody, guilt-ridden role. It's a play-of-the-week starring Cyril Cusack and Joan McKenna. Can you hear the uillean pipes?'

'Siobhan McKenna. Anyway nothing's decided.'

'Don't. Everything is decided. We've been all around the houses with this, it's set for Tuesday. We do it and it's done.'

'I'm the one up on the table!'

'Woosums! So fine, okay. Tell you what. Let's have it then. We'll buy a semi-d and sign up for Fianna Fail.'

'You're an arse. Why don't you go and rub off Mary Pearson some more?'

'Maybe I shall, maybe I shall,' and he made the cross-eyed look, and he did the Twilight Zone music, and she laughed.

'What are we going to do, Jack?'

'Another half?'

'Unbelievable! Really, I mean you're outdoing yourself tonight.'

'I know. I'm a maggot. And you adore me, so deal with it. And come here, look? Please.'

She could taste a mercury note in her mouth and she wondered if this was in some way connected. She rose to leave. She was quickly getting towards the end of Jack. She saw that all was used to reinforce his masculine place in the world. All was weighed and tested for advantage. In everything that occurred, he saw possibilities for developing his own sense of himself: he had used the crisis merely to give a burnish to his self-importance.

'Where you going?'

'Stay where you are, Jack, I'm just getting some water. I'll be a second.'

Everytime she left his presence she felt a delicious lightness come on her. She went lightly down the stairs and into the late throb of the party. The house was full of music and breathless talk and attempted romance but just as it peaked it began to fade, too, and people were tiring some, they were beginning to splay out on the cushions on the floor. The cheap drugs were wearing off and Sunday morning had begun to announce itself. It threw rain against the windows, like handfuls of gravel and nails, and there was stomach cramp and dryness of the mouth and morbid thoughts. Serotonin receptors tipped over like skittles—dead. Kay went to find her coat. The coats were in a pile behind the record decks and she winked at the dour-faced Northerner playing records.

'Kay, what about you?' he said.

'Alright, Coll?'

His world was round, twelve inches in circumference, and made out of black vinyl. He had tight hair composed of tiny curls and he would take a curl and twiggle it between thumb and forefinger, a nervous tic. His calling was to educate the west of Ireland to the pleasures of old-skool Detroit techno. The trouble with this town was that people didn't want to know. They wanted to listen to the same old same old, week in week out. They wanted the big tunes. They wanted the cheese. Well, they could look elsewhere. He wasn't going to play ball. If they didn't like it, they could piss off. If they wanted cheese, they could go down and listen to Sonny Byrne. They'd deserve each other, Sonny Byrne and that crowd. Fucking mouth-breathers the pack of them.

'Do you know what I'm saying, Kay?'

But she was gone, she'd headed for the door, in a swish of auburn hair and a fun-fur coat. Little Miss Thing. Not that the thought hadn't crossed his mind. What she was doing with the other creature he would never know. Jack Keohane? An excuse for humanity! An egomaniac! But that was this town all over, wasn't it? It was all surface. Sometimes he wondered why he troubled himself with these people at all. They hadn't a notion. To prove the point, he put on an old Derrick May, one of the first Rhythm Is Rhythm things—genius!—and he surveyed the room owlishly as it kicked in, but no. They didn't get it. He twiggled a tiny curl between thumb and forefinger. He chewed a lip and sulked. He had enough of the place. He was going to take off, no question, one of these fine days, they wouldn't see his arse for dust. They'd be sorry then, and they listening to Sonny Byrne and his cheese—big fucking piano tunes. The major problem would be the shipment of the records. There were several thousand and that amounted to serious dead weight. Everybody was sprawled and splayed, they were lying wrapped around each other on the floor. A handful of gravel against the window. He'd just put on an Orb album and leave it at that. It was as much as they deserved. He went through to the kitchen to search out

Noreen. There was no sign of Noreen.

'Nice set, Coll,' said Helen.

'Oh was it?' he said, 'was it really now? So what the fuck are you doing in here?'

She huffed out of the kitchen. The sooner somebody took that arsehole to one side and sorted him out, the better. Helen Coyle, if she insisted on anything, insisted that life should be mannerly. She was a petite dark-haired girl, carefully arranged, with an expression of tremendous pleasantness and openness. She thrived on neatness in all things. She had been at a loss, tonight, when she realised that her affairs had spun out of control. She was in the process of leaving Eoin for James. She sat on the stairs and reviewed the situation. She had not quite informed either of her plans. She felt that she had put enough out in the way of suggestion and signals, that they should each be able to grasp the new reality.

Dealing with men was like dealing with infants. If they weren't puppy-dog, they were crude and arrogant, and which was worse? She wasn't ever taking ecstasy again. It brought all this emotional crap up. And it… just… wasn't… neat. She put her head against the banisters and closed her eyes. Eoin, in her opinion, had already stalled in life. When they first went out, he'd seemed to have every-thing opening up for him. He was rangy, good-looking, quick-wit-ted, he was fit and active, he didn't drink much or smoke much or do drugs much, he was sociable and presentable. But slowly, in the two years of their relationship, his terrible secret had slipped out: he was a settler. He would settle for the small solicitors firm in Galway. He would settle for a quiet, unperturbed life. He would settle for a house on Taylor's Hill and a new Saab on a biannual basis, and he would involve himself delicately in the probate of small farmers and shopkeepers, and he would father unassuming and well-spoken children. But not with Helen Coyle he wouldn't.

James, who was, inevitably, Eoin's best friend, had a wider reach to his ambition. He was a broad-beamed, meat-faced man—at just twenty-two, there was none of the boy left—and he moved across the ground with a sure-footedness born of privilege. He had subtly courted Helen Coyle for the two years she had been involved with his friend—in the end, not all that subtly—because he had recognised early that in back of the pleasantness and openness there was an overwhelming want for progress. He saw that they would propel each other forward, through all the years and the bunfights, that neither would allow the other to slacken, not for a moment. James was handsome but in the way that a bulldog is handsome and in the cause of advancement he would have the grip and clench of a bulldog's jaws. That was good enough for Helen Coyle—she'd made her decision.

Slowly, with a sense of building unease, the night gave away on itself. The slow fog of the mood drugs lifted and left nothing at all behind. Still there was some low music and people lay on the cushions and couches, and Alice, button-nosed, slept on her arms at the kitchen table. There was a tiny snoring sound if you crept up and listened to her quietly, and she dreamt of faraway places and pleasant young men in a warm light.

The nineteen year old from Roscommon had been rebuffed at every turn and he prepared for a cold wet walk out the long curve of the bay to Salthill. He would not spend on a taxi if there wasn't cause to. They would already be unwrapping bundles of newspapers outside the churches and the gulls, raucous with winter, would circle down from the low sky in search of last night's chips.

Helen went to her room upstairs and she quickly, neatly undressed and she stood for a moment with her left hand laid on her flawless belly—the satisfaction of that—and her pert nose twitched, she believed that she could smell smoke. She put on her dressing gown and followed the smell, it came from down the hallway, from the boxroom. She pushed in the door and saw Jack asleep on the narrow bed and the filthy old carpet smouldering on the floor. It was clear at a glance what had happened. His cigarette had fallen but there had been a piece of luck, he had the window open and rain had come in and put out the few flames that had started. It was almost at the finish of its damp smouldering by now. She went to find Coll, who shared the house, and yeah, a bucket of water, just to be sure. Fucking Jack! He could have put the whole place up, these old houses were always going up. Every year the *Advertiser* had another dreary tragedy, with names and ages and places of origin, from Carlow, originally, from Roscommon, originally.

Coll was back in the living room, flicking through his records. She whispered it to him. Fucksake! he said. Fucking typical of these people! There's another deposit gone! He ran upstairs and saw that it was as she said—he didn't and never would trust women's accounts of things—and he went to fetch the water. When she had bent down to whisper to him, he turned just in time to see the swell of a breast beneath the dressing gown and the image now occupied his mind to a far greater degree than the non-event of a failed fire.

Martina turned to Mary Pearson, on a couch pushed back to the living-room wall, and she said:

'Dave Costelloe? Yeah, but… kind of low-sized, isn't he?'

'I know. It's the kind of way that if he was three inches taller he'd be a different man.'

'Yeah but I do know what you mean, he's kind of dirty?'

'Oh, filthy! There is absolute filth in those eyes.'

'Yeah, there is but… Jesus. Can you believe the time?'

'Sunday's a write-off. Come here, do you want to go and get some breakfast? I'm pretty sure Anton's is open.'

It was eight o'clock, in Galway, on a Sunday morning. The wind had eased, to some extent. It would be a cold day with intermittent rain. Ollie drove the Corolla down the docks, his beany head swivelling left and right. He had people to see at the Harbour Bar, which kept market hours, and he had only the one wiper working. In rain, it felt as though the Corolla was gone half-blind. His shin was reefed open from the drainpipe but the wound had dried up some and, all told, it was unlikely to kill him. He passed by the house and wondered if there was anything still going on there. If things worked out at the Harbour Bar, he could knock back up and do some more business. But just as he drove past, the last of the stragglers emerged to the grey old streets and another wet morning of the reconstruction.

Breakfast Wine

They say it takes just three alcoholics to keep a small bar running in a country town and while myself and the cousin, Thomas, were doing what we could, we were a man shy, and these were difficult days for Mr Kelliher, licencee of The North Star, Pearse Street.

'The next thing an ESB bill will come lording in the door to me,' he said. 'That could tip me over the edge altogether. Or wait until you see, the fucker for the insurance will arrive in. Roaring.'

He took the rag to the counter and worked the rag in small tight circles, worked it with the turn of the knot and the run of the grain, he was a man of precise small flourishes, Mr Kelliher, and these flourishes were a taunt to the world. Even in desperate times, they said, proper order shall be maintained. The Kelliher mouth, like generations of Kelliher mouths before it, was bitter, dry and clamped, and the small grey eyes were deranged with injustice.

'I've no cover,' he said. 'My arse is hanging out to an extraordinary degree. I'm open to the fates. It's myself and the four winds. You'll see me yet, boys, with a suitcase, at the side of the road, and the long face on. The workhouse! That's what they'll have to get going again for the likes of me.'

The clock considered twelve and passed it by with a soft shudder, as though it had been a close call. It seemed to be a fine enough day, out there beyond the blinds. Birds in the trees and flowers in the park and the first bit of warmth of the year. The torpid movement of late morning in the town, and the sunlight harsh in its vitality, as if it was only here to show the place up.

'Nail me to a cross and crucify me,' said Mr Kelliher, 'and at least that way I'd go quick.'

The North Star was an intimate place, a place of dark wood and polished optics, with the radio tuned to the classical station for calm (it played lowly, very lowly) and the blinds let slants of light in and you'd see distant to the morbid hills, if you strained yourself. Myself and Thomas were sat there on the high stools. We were fine specimens of bile and fear and broken sleep. There was slow hungry slurping, and I finished what was before me.

'Would you put on a pint for me, Mr Kelliher?'

'I would of course, Brendan.'

'Cuz?'

'I will so,' said Thomas.

Mr Kelliher never drank himself—not anymore—but he drank milky tea by the gallon, and a whistling kettle was kept in perpetual operation in the small private space adjoining the bar. Its whistle was a lonesome gull, or the wheeze of a lung, and it was part of the music of the house. Mr Kelliher attended to the stout. Each fresh glass he filled two sevenths shy of the brim, with the glass delicately inclined towards the pourer's breast, so as the stout would not injure itself with a sheer fall, and he set them then, and there was the rush and mingle of brown and cream notes, and the blackness rising, a magic show you would never tire of.

'Small industry in this country is being wiped out,' said Mr Kelliher.

'Who are you telling?' I said.

'It's the likes of us who toil and scrape, Brendan. We're the ones getting a clatter off the blunt end of a spade. Ignorance! That's all you come up against around this place.'

'Shocking,' I agreed.

He removed our used glasses—averting his eyes from them, so decorous—and placed them in the neat dishwasher, where they would expect company. He filled to the top the fresh ones and with a curt nod put them before us and a note was slid across and we moved our lips wordlessly in thanks.

'There are fellas in Leinster House would shame a brothel,' he said.

We had no women. It was an awful lack in our lives. Mothers, daughters, lovers, wives, we had none of these at all, not a one between us, because women were a premium in the county, and in truth we were hardly prizetakers. It was from this lack of women that we had turned into auld women ourselves. Daily we regaled each other with our ailments and complaints, we talked of changes in the weather, and strangers in the town. Nothing could occur in the town of an insignificance beyond our gossip. If a wall got a lick of paint, it would be remarked in The North Star. Mr Kelliher winced, and stretched a liver-spotted hand up behind himself to investigate a region of the upper back, and his eyes leapt to the ceiling, and he said:

'Would you ever get a class of a cold pain out a lung?'

'Would you not mean a kind of a white heat, Mr Kelliher?'

'Precisely so, Brendan!'

'Searing,' said Thomas.

'Like a poker!' said Mr Kelliher.

'Arra,' I said, and we all three of us nodded in sad resignation.

The North Star was discreetly situated in the town. You trailed down the steep decline of Russell Hill, passed Bord Gáis and Hair Affair, you kept your head down passing the guards, you moved away from the commerce and traffic of the town, you hung an abrupt left into a narrow, vague, nothing-much sort of a street, and this was Pearse Street, its dullness a measure of the low esteem that particular martyr was held in hereabouts. The North Star was the only action on Pearse Street, and sunlight breached this narrow gorge for just one hour a day but now was the hour and Mr Kelliher came out from behind the bar and he shut the blinds fully against it. He was a small man neatly hewn, and sallow, with impressively planed features, like the carved dark aztec of a cliff-face, and he was of indeterminate age, it wouldn't surprise you if he was forty-three or seventy-four, and there was something of Charlie Chaplin in the swing-along, quick-stepping gait, but you wouldn't mention it.

'Turned out fairly nice, Mr Kelliher.'

'Pleasant enough looking, Brendan.'

'After the night we put down.'

'Sure the night was filthy altogether.'

He picked up the neatly placed beer mats from each of The North Star's five zinc-topped tables, though they hadn't been used, and he replaced them with fresh, which he dealt out with Vegas flourish. Stepped in behind the bar again, with a clearing of the throat, hmm-hmm, and it was the satisfaction of small rituals that emanated from him, though by now it was a weakish glow.

'What way are they above?'

'Well, Mr Kelliher.'

'That's good at least. Did you tell them Hourigan was gone to the wall?'

'I did.'

'They'd have sport from that?'

'They would, Mr Kelliher.'

'A very bleak situation.'

'I thought he had his head above water.'

'Indeed no.'

'Hard to have sympathy, all the same?'

'Same fella wouldn't piss on you, Brendan.'

'The beard does nothing for him,' said Thomas.

The classical music succumbed to a news bulletin and there was talk of violent death, atrocities in Africa, oil shortages, a widow in Castleisland with lucky numbers for the Lottery, and we listened, keenly enough, for The North Star was at a remove from the world, certainly, but by no means cut off from it.

'A sad, peculiar life, gentlemen?'

'To put it very mildly, Mr Kelliher.'

The stout was about its work. It was the third drink of the day, and the drinking would slow now to session pace—the dread of the morning had lifted, we had passed the hour of remorse, and we marched to the mellow afternoon. Even Thomas was starting to look fairly chipper. A strange rumbling then, like dogs going at each other in the distance, but it was internal, miserably, and I wasn't sure if it was my own stomach or the cousin's. Serious drinking, the drinking of a lifetime's devotion, is hard physical labour.

'You persevere despite it all, Mr Kelliher?'

'You never weaken, Brendan. Weaken and all is lost.'

It was due that the crossword of the *Irish Times* would put in an appearance, and the three of us would make light work of it, normally. Thomas would be an amazement to you. Sit there like a stone all the morning and then start throwing out words like 'inimical' and 'hauteur'. But the crossword was left aside, for there was to be a disturbance this day in The North Star. The door opened up, and glamour stepped in.

Glamour carried itself with great elegance and ease. It was jewelled at the fingers and jewelled at the throat. It wore fine woolens and high leather boots and a green velvet cape, the texture such an excitement against machine-tanned skin. Glamour took onto a high stool beside us, and delicately arranged itself.

'Howye, lads,' she said. 'What reds have ye on?'

The North Star was by no means inoculated against the charms of glamour, especially when it spoke with this whispery hoarseness, and Mr Kelliher was a flushed boy as he pressed into action.

'Madam,' he said. 'I'm afraid I can only offer a meagre selection. But let's see now, let's see.'

He took down one each of the varieties of red wine he kept in the house, the little 33cl, glass-and-a-bit bottles, which myself and Thomas sometimes resorted to late in the evening, if the sheer volume of stout was threatening to overwhelm matters. The evenings we hit the firewater are as well left unremarked.

'Really,' said Mr Kelliher, 'I should put you in the hands of these gentlemen. They'd be the experts.'

I nodded, shyly, and reached down to see if my voice would function, and it had a quiver and a quake but it emerged anyway.

'The merlot isn't a bad old drop, as it goes,' I said. 'A Chilean.'

'Oh?' she said, and she took the bottle to examine it. She granted a familiar smile to me, and she crossed her long legs beneath the woolen folds. The electric rustling of nylons was heard, it went off like a crack of lightning in the premises, and a light sweat broke out on my forehead.

'The pinot noir is bog standard, to be honest with you. It'd be fairly... flat, really. Of the three, I'd nearly go for the cabarnet. It's not going to stand up and talk to you, it's very much the usual, but there's nothing wrong with that. It's kinda...'

'Full and ripe?' she said, with the mouth twisted slightly.

'You could say.'

'A very nice breakfast wine,' said Thomas, you'd never know when he was going to come out with a quick one. She granted to him a slyer smile.

'I'll take your word for it,' she said, and she took the bottle and unscrewed the top, the movement of her long fingers was quick and dizzying.

Now jealousy was no stranger in the town. It was my own foul weather, a cold mist that surrounded me. But it's a familiar old song, that one, you'd hear it in every public bar of the town, you'd hear it in all the low bars of Nicholas Street, and in the suede-smelling hush of the hotel's lounge bar, you'd hear it in all the honky tonks of the Castle Walk. The radio announced that a complex frontal trough was moving in off the Atlantic. Good luck to it.

'The sort of day,' she said, 'you wouldn't know would you want a coat on you or what. Seasons changing.'

'They haven't much choice,' said Mr Kelliher. 'Where are you from yourself?'

She named a western town, a place so far away that we hadn't a picture at all of the fallings of life in that town, though we'd suspect them to be harsh.

'And what brings you here?' said Mr Kelliher.

'A minor secondary road,' she said, and winked him one, and he lit up like Christmas.

She enquired about rental accommodation in the town, and I could sense stirrings the other side of me on a high stool. We related to her what possibilities there were.

'Are you talking a night or a week or what?'

'You wouldn't know,' she said. 'I'm the way I don't know how a notion might turn in me. Did you ever get that way? Did you ever wake up and think, what about a turn on the heel? What about a sudden swerve?'

She seemed carefully made up, at first glance, but a more considered examination, there in the convivial afternoon of The North Star, revealed the flaws and slips. The mascara had run a little at the eyes, and the lip gloss was a rush job, and this gave her a fraught quality. It hinted at drama that was by no means unwelcome, for the days were slow in The North Star, and the nights were only trotting after them.

'Would you put on a pint for me, Mr Kelliher?'

'I would, Brendan.'

'Cuz?'

'Go on sure.'

'And yourself, miss?'

'Very kind,' she said.

Mr Kelliher smirked in the way that he has.

'Very poor qualities of observation I would have to say, Brendan.'

'Oh?'

'This isn't a miss we have,' and he wriggled fingers in the air, and I caught it, belatedly, on the third finger of her left hand, the sparkler. She looked at it herself and mock-proudly held it for display.

'Actually,' she said, 'I'm separated.'

A class of dizziness palpable from the high stool the other side of me.

'I'm sorry to hear that,' whispered Mr Kelliher, decorous again after his cheeky intrusion.

'Ah,' she said. 'It's the way things work out sometimes.'

We nodded, the three men, sombre as owls. We nodded as though the cruel variables of love were hardly news to us. We nodded as though we'd each known heartbreak and the ache of a lost love, as though we'd each walked the Castle Walk, at four in the morning, in cold rain, with the collars turned up against a lonely wind. Oh what we wouldn't have given for broken hearts.

'A marriage is an old record,' she said. 'It'll go around and

around grand for years and then it gets so scratched it's unlisten-
able.'

Stranger talk, this, and there was unease now at the counter of
The North Star. Even before our stout was settled and served, she
was making good progress on the second small bottle of cabernet.

'Are ye farming, men?' she said.

'You'd hardly call it that,' I said, 'at this stage.'

'Site farmers!' said Mr Kelliher.

'Don't mind him,' I said.

'You take what's going,' she said.

'A fool not to,' I said.

Certainly, these had been good years for us. The land of the
vicinity wasn't great, not by any stretch, but it had fine views of
dreary hills, and the rivers were swollen with licey trout, and this
was enough to draw people in. We sold them what space they wanted, having plenty to spare.

A truck went past, rattling the neat stacks of glasses, and Mr Kelliher
shut his eyes, briefly, in suffering, and he was seen to suppress a
swear.

'More of it,' he said. 'They're using it as a rat run, d'you see?
Since they got in the traffic calming up on the Castle Walk. Bastards
of lorries cutting down all day, you'll pardon my French. What way
are ye over for traffic calming?'

'Measures are in place,' she said. 'But if you're asking me if any
good is being done?'

She shrugged. It was an expansive movement, performed, to let
us know in the cheap seats that a wry puzzlement was signalled. She
was a kind of woman not entirely unknown to us. In quietish towns,
there are women with a great want for drama and heat, even if it's
only trouble that can bring it. Such a woman might often be the only
throb of life in a place. We were stirred by her. Mr Kelliher's mouth
hung on its hinges and waves of emotion swept over him, as though
she was a sacred daughter brought back from the wolves. Thomas,
by the big red face on him, was clearly subject to notions himself.
And I couldn't wait to get home so as I could dream about her.

'Take all the cars off the roads,' she said. 'All the trucks and all the jeeps. Build bonfires of the things and torch them. Watch them burn, wait for the tanks to blow. Storm the county councils and rip up the road plans. No more roundabouts and no more lay-bys. Anybody stepping anywhere near a vehicle of any mechanical description is put up against a wall and shot before night. Imagine it, lads—the world slows again to a human pace. We could saunter and stroll. How would that be?'

'A woman,' said Thomas, 'after my own heart.'

'Mind you,' she said, and she held three fingers aloft, indicated with them our glasses, and winked for Mr Kelliher. 'I was thankful for the car under me when I was putting distance between myself and Rhino Flynn.'

'Who?'

'My husband,' she said.

'And ye're... separated now?'

'We are,' she said. 'Since about half four this morning.'

She drained what was left of the second cabernet, made a start on the fresh. From a wallet of fine snakeskin she placed a note on the table.

'One yourself, sir?'

'Thanks, I won't,' said Mr Kelliher. 'I haven't drank in years.'

'Oh?'

'It wasn't agreeing with me. A doctor put me on the spot and said I wouldn't see forty.'

'And now you've seen it,' she said, 'has it been worth it?'

'Arguable,' he said.

We went uncertainly into the afternoon. The classical station went into its period of great torpor, to the slowest dirges and dreamiest movements. Up top of the hill, the town could be heard to go about its Thursday business. Car doors slamming was the punctuation of the place. Soon enough, they'd let out from the primary school, and quick giddy footsteps would go past outside, and sing-song taunts in unbroken voices. We knew them all. We'd watch them grow taller and leave. The years come in, the years go out. The longer you'd sit and look at it, the life of the town would contract to almost nothing, to the merest glimpse of life, the tiniest crack of light against the black. It passes quickest in the slow places.

'You'd hear him before you'd see him,' she said. 'Big old lunk. Big shit head on him. Powerful build of a man but a small child at the end of the day.'

'Would be often the way, missus.'

'You can call me Josie,' she said, and the name was all her, it had carnival roll to it, and more drinks were arranged.

'I don't know would I have a Heineken?' she said. 'I have a throat on me but no, listen, I'll stick with these. Grape or grain, never the twain.'

'Hard-won wisdom,' I said.

'Married at all yereselves, lads?' she said. 'I didn't think so. Ye're as well not. Less complications.'

'I could use complications,' said Thomas.

'Now!' said Mr Kelliher. 'That's a ripe one, Tom.'

Thomas slugged off the high stool, he was embarrassed once the words slipped out, and he headed for the gents. She watched him over her shoulder, the tip of her tongue emerging between her lips.

'What's with the quiet man?' she said.

'The strong silent type,' said Mr Kelliher.

'Learned my lesson about them longo,' she said.

I felt a thrumming within myself, the heartbeat had quickened, and Mr Kelliher worked the rag with the turn of the knot and the run of the grain, and we were nervous until Thomas got back.

'So tell me,' she said. 'Is it always this hectic?'

She crossed and uncrossed her legs, there was a crack of lightning, and the afternoon was in around me like redcoats with muskets primed, and I said:

'Would you put on a pint for me, Mr Kelliher?'

'I would, Brendan.'

'Cuz?'

'Would you ever leave me live my fucking life?' said Thomas.

'He will, Mr Kelliher. Josie?'

'One for the high road,' she said.

Things settled again, and cream notes mingled with brown, and though I searched for the small talk that might work as lead to weight the balloon, there wasn't need for it, because something had given away in Josie now: she showed herself more fully.

'Strain in my neck from the car,' she said. 'Driving half the night on bad roads. But I had to get away from the other bastard. The poison got into the big fool and he couldn't let me out of his sight. The next thing I know I'm on the floor of the garage tied down with flex.'

The schoolchildren passed by outside, high and excited, the sense of release, the daily fiesta of half past three, and the town's noises would change and quicken with the afternoon, a particular agitation would surface, the rush and hubbub of it, people hurrying home to whatever was waiting, and normally at this time the pace of our drinking would quicken also. Often, it was the hour of the firewater.

'This is what flex does,' she said, and she shucked the cuffs of her sleeves to show the weals and the raised welts, blistered yellow and furious red, and soft consoling noises were made. Grip her gently in the darkness, pull her towards you: it would read like Braille.

'Who were you talking to, he says. I seen you talking to him. Why were you talking to him…' She shrugged it away. 'I should have seen it coming.'

She finished what was left of her drink, and she regarded us with great fondness and there was an intimation that there was shared history to come, that she too would become a familiar of the premises.

'It's been something else, fellas,' she said, and she carried herself to the door on careful heels, not a single step was sloppily placed.

'I open at eleven,' said Mr Kelliher, discreetly.

'Good to know,' she winked for him once more, and left.

So it was that The North Star was saved. With its five zinc-topped tables in the afternoon gloom, and the pendant flags of Tipperary, the gold and the blue, and its three high stools placed so by the bar. The turn of the dark wood's knot, the run of its grain. The shine of the optics, the calender, the lulling music always played. The North Star is immune to all winds and complex troughs. The North Star, a safe haven.

Burn The Bad Lamp

A man walks into a corner shop. He is a nervous man, easily knocked from his groove, and it is a great disturbance to him when he is addressed by a four foot tall chicken.

'Cluckety cluck,' it says. 'Try your luck?'

Ralph Coughlan and the chicken have this encounter six days a week and it's doing neither of them any favours. He knows there is a motion sensor embedded behind the chicken's eyes that clocks his movement. He is quite aware that it is an electronic chicken that lays plastic eggs containing trinkets and toys but even so, it leaves him a little shook. It's got to the stage where he is trying to tiptoe past the chicken to dodge the sensor's reach. It is a Tuesday, in March, with all that that suggests. Ralph scans the magazine racks as he waits to be served. All the magazines are about extreme sports and cannabis cultivation techniques. The shop is operated by an unpleasantly owl-faced woman. Not once in four years has he had even a suggestion of warmth from this person. He knows that 'perceived slights' is one of the key danger signs but there is nothing perceived about it. He is always super-friendly himself, to provide an instructive contrast with her surliness, but you might as well instruct the wall. He buys a sausage roll, a Diet Coke, and a scratchcard. She slams his change onto the counter and eyes him as though to say, more? Is there something more?

'Ferocious day alright,' he says. 'But typical enough for March, I suppose?'

'Yeah?'

'That's a breeze would take skin off you.'

'Is it?'

He goes to sit on a bench that overlooks one of the river's drearier stretches. They have some cheek putting a bench down here. It is a most exposed spot and there isn't a day you get up off this bench you're not red in the face from wind. There is drizzle and general damp. It's the sort of town that would give you a chest infection. He eats his lunch. He scratches away the useless card. He wonders about the latest knot in his gut and the new tremble that's put in an appearance on his upper lip.

Ralph's is a hard-luck street down by the quays. There is, more often than not, a dead dog in the gutter. A man behind a pram waits for the lights and coos over his baby. Outside the off-licence, some haughty drunks contest the hold of a bottle. It is a place for connoisseurs of the forlorn and the shop fronts are painted in carnival colours. Ralph bins his trash and crosses the road to his place of business. He is subject to seething monotones and moments of glow.

Someone has left a box in the doorway. This bugs him, big time. People think they can treat Coughlan's like a charity shop. They say hey, listen, okay, what we'll do? We'll drop it off with the guy down the quay, the guy with the hair. Ralph drags the box into the shop and kicks it to one side. He becomes philosophical then—at least the box can occupy a segment of his Wednesday. Ralph divides his days into segments, with each segment defined by a designated task.

The next segment is marked down for polishing. They aren't exactly beating down the door but that's no reason to let things go. When the customers do arrive, Coughlan's will be looking as well as it has any right to look. Ralph has a selection of chamois leathers for polishing. He has great belief in the restorative powers of a shammy. He feels a measure of happiness as he polishes but tries not to notice it. Ralph stocks select pieces of second-hand furniture, some antiques, and smaller items that could be classed only as ornaments. He sources from auction rooms, clearance sales and the more distant coves of e-bay. Ralph's shop is in the wrong part of town. It has dawned on him that there isn't much of an incidental trade for antiques and ornaments down here. He polishes a brass monocular that has been in the shop since day one. It is an excellent monocular, in fine working nick, and well priced. What could be more convenient for the casual birder out for a peep at the oystercatchers in Crosshaven of a Sunday? But there's a problem, Ralph realises, with monoculars. People feel stupid using them. They feel like they're playing at being Jack Palance in a pirate film.

Ralph polishes a vintage dairy urn. He is having his doubts about the vintage dairy urn. His initial feeling was that it might appeal to sentimental people who had background in the country, that it would make a talking point in a hall, but there aren't many sentimental people on the ground lately. He runs a cloth over a very nice telephone table. It is a lovely piece, with a built-in stool and a neat slot for a phone book. It has a racy, late '50s air, practical yet stylish. You could see an elegant lady sat down at it, with the legs crossed, taking a call. Ralph can almost hear the rustle of her nylons. She's in a pair of kitten heels and Cary Grant is at the other end of the line.

Ralph's polishing takes on the heat of frenzy. He does a mantel clock he bought from the tinkers in Bantry, then a selection of Ardagh crystal pieces, then some Victorian doorknobs. He squidgees the windows. He has a panic attack of middling intensity—it feels like some cats have got loose inside his chest—and he clutches at a rad for support. He has run out of things to polish. There's nothing for it but to open the box that was left in the doorway. It is the kind of day a man is well advised to keep busy.

It's mostly junk. A scratched magnifying glass, old paperbacks, a wooden jewellery case with carved elephants and inside a legend scrawled in black marker—'Patricia Loves Bay City Rollers'—and he can see her, with wispy hair and a gammy eye, her spectacles held with cellotape in 1974. A figurine of a pissing boy, an imitation Wedgwood plate, more paperbacks, but then a nice old oil lamp, with a brass frame surrounding a smoky brown glass. Ralph fills it with the paraffin he keeps in the shop for just this purpose. Nostalgic people like oil lamps, and he has sold a few. The wick takes nicely but the flame shows up some smears on the brown glass. Ralph takes a shammy to the glass and polishes it carefully.

A genie appears.

The manner of the apparition is much as we have been led to expect. There is a puff of purple smoke and a male figure floats up out of the lamp in a comfortably cross-legged sitting pose, like a man who has put the hours in on the yoga mat. But then the smoke clears and the genie separates from legend. There are no tapered slippers nor flowing silks. He wears no turban, nor fathomless expression. He wears a pair of troubled chinos, an overcoat with fag burns on its lapels, a pair of scuffed Nikes and a leery, self-satisfied smirk. He's one of those small butty fellas, fortyish, thinning up top, and the bit of hair that's left could usefully be introduced to a bottle of Head 'n' Shoulders.

'How'd you like this for caper?' he says.

'Listen,' says Ralph. 'I can't be dealing with this kind of messin'. I'm on tablets, like.'

'Relax,' says the genie. 'Just try and calm yourself, okay? The last thing we want is you on the flat of your back outside in the Regional. Have a sit down, Mr Coughlan. Take it easy.'

The genie sits at the telephone table. He primly lifts an imagined receiver, with his pinkie finger cocked.

'Hallooo?' he says. 'Hallooooo? Coughlan's?'

He takes out a packet of Rothmans, lights one, then lets up a terrible, wracking cough.

'It's these fuckers have me nearly murdered, Ralph,' he says.

Ralph goes behind his counter and pops an emergency beta-blocker.

'You want to clear out of here now,' he says, 'or I'll call the guards.'

'And you're going to say what, Ralph?'

Ralph's eyes water up. His voice becomes scratchy and gasped.

'What are you doing here?' he says.

'Come on,' says the genie. 'You know the script, Ralph. I'm after floating out of a lamp, aren't I? You know what comes next.'

'But why are you *here*?'

The genie grins, and he begins to pace the floor, with his hands held casually behind his back.

'It's nearly always a lamp with me,' he says, 'but then again, I'm one of life's traditionalists. There are others who have taken a completely different approach. You can understand how a young man coming into the field would be keen to adopt his own method. There's one guy who pops up out of a toaster. There's another fella appears like an air bag if you brake suddenly at a certain junction on a particular country road. Now if you ask me, that's acting the maggot. You could give someone heart failure. And between myself, yourself and the wall, there's been a couple of very sad cases.'

'You mean to tell me,' says Ralph, 'that people have actually...'

'All I'll say, Ralph, is that our health-and-safety record isn't all it could be.'

Ralph eyes this genie carefully. Ralph has a couple of difficult years put down, a time when his old certainties went tumbling, and anything that smells of opportunity he views balefully now, a once-bitten man.

'Listen,' he says, 'do you always deal with local cases yourself?'

'Mostly,' says the genie. 'The odd time I knock up and cover for a guy in Tipp. He comes down bad with hay fever around May, June, when they're turning up fields. And I tell you, Ralph, it's no joke dealing with the crowd up there. The country people have turned most avaricious in recent times.'

'So what exactly is the deal here? I get three wishes, is that what you're saying?'

'Correct.'

'And it doesn't matter what they are?'

'I wouldn't go that far. I can be as disappointed in people as the next man. And if I'm disappointed, who's to say that I'll perform my duties in as careful a manner as I should? Try not to disappoint me, Ralph. I hate to be disappointed in people. Would you believe I'd a guy wishing for a long-term parking space convenient to the South Mall? I had another fella looking for a 48-inch plasma screen. I looked at him, Ralph, and I said what do you think you're dealing with here, an Argos catalogue?'

The genie becomes irate. The pitch of his voice rises.

'You give people a chance!' he says, balling a fist and slapping it into his palm. 'You give them a chance to transform their lives! You give people possibilities! You give them every fucking opportunity. And what do they do? They look at you like you're crazy. Don't disappoint me, Ralph.'

'I wish,' says Ralph Coughlan, 'that I had a singing voice.'

The genie stops short.

'I see,' he says. 'And how long have you been having problems at home?'

Ralph pales:

'What do you mean?'

'All the old spark gone out of it, killer?'

This Coughlan case, thinks the genie, is a no-brainer. When a man starts wishing for the power of song, it is a general fact that he is trying to impress women.

'I don't know what you're talking about,' says Ralph. 'Look, can you do it for me or not? What I'd love is a good, solid tenor, one that'll hold through on a note, but if that's too much to ask, maybe you could just do me something that's kinda… husky?'

The genie holds up a warning palm.

'Wait,' he says. 'Let me think this over.'

The genie settles on a seventies sofa chair of brown corduroy, crosses his short legs, and considers the ramifications of Ralph Coughlan's wish. You can't just suddenly give someone a singing voice and forget all about it. You have to consider what they'll do with this gift because our talents, coldly used, can be deadly as knives. The genie notes that Ralph is a dapper sort: he is well-turned out, carefully groomed. Also there is the fact of the hair. The genie has to be careful. This could be like turning a young Engelbert Humperdinck loose on the northside of the city. There wouldn't be a marriage safe for miles.

It is in this way that the genie's job sometimes has a high stress level. You will already have met genies, at flotation centres, at reiki workshops, haunting the backs of chapels, trying everything and anything as they attempt to ease their anxieties. You will see them slumped over tables in sad dockside bars, or waiting on prescriptions in late-night pharmacies. Many avail of early-retirement packages but even if they leave the service at fifty they are already, in many cases, broken men. The manipulation and shaping of dreams can really take it out of you.

'Well?' says Ralph.

'Un momento, por favor,' says the genie.

Rush hour thickens on the quay outside. There is general belligerence. Men parp their horns at each other. Seabirds jacked up on weird emissions from the chemical plants downriver stand with deranged eyes on the quayside walls and seem to waver in the light breeze and they watch it all go by.

Now what if a singing Ralph proves to be a force for good in his community? The genie pictures Ralph appearing at fundraisers for Nigerian refugees, or launching into feel-good John Denver numbers on Sunday morning visits to the terminally ill.

Ralph waits. He looks at the genie with a coolness now. This genie, it is Ralph's opinion, could use a good wet shave. Ralph will never present himself to the world with an unclean jaw. He will appear to a room with a suave smile and a small bow, in a well-pressed suit, with lightly dressed hair, and he will begin to softly croon. The room will be packed with doe-eyed lovelies. They will all but have to be shovelled out of the seats.

'No rush, genie,' he says.

The genie retains some sympathy for his client. He's just one of these big handsome fools, the type of man who believes that if he keeps brushing his teeth and thinking pretty thoughts, it'll all turn out gravy.

'Okay. We're going to do it, Ralph. You can sing.'

Ralph emits a small, delighted gasp and gets to his feet. The rolodex in his brain flips over and over and searches through all the easy-listening finger clickers he's ever been partial to and stops at the Ws: he selects 'Can't Get Used To Losing You' by Andy Williams.

'Guess there's no use in hangin' rouuuuund,' he begins. 'Guess I'll get dressed and do the towwwwn.'

He still sounds like something off a turkey farm. The genie is sombre.

'I can hear where you're coming from, Ralphie.'

'What's the story, like?'

'Not always instantaneous,' says the genie. 'Relax. The docket is gone in. A lot of these things we can do on the spot but there are others that take a little time. You'll know when it's there for you. Trust me.'

'I'm starting to have my doubts here,' says Ralph Coughlan.

The genie's superiors consider the case. They raise their eyebrows. They know that for the Ralph Coughlans of this world, things can go either way. The slightest intervention and your Ralph Coughlan has a suitcase on the bed and a taxi called for the station. He's thinking, will I bring a towel or will they have towels there?

Ralph and the genie observe the city groaning past outside. The traffic is choked, and it's warm for March, the car windows are rolled down and you can hear all the radios. A headbanger on a death metal show responds to a texted request: Sorry, girl, he says, I got nothin' with me by Slayer.

'Let's do it again, Ralph,' says the genie. 'Let's do it so we can get home to our teas.'

Ralph Coughlan is troubled. Small worms of concentration wriggle on his brow.

'Listen,' he says. 'What kind of thing do people ask for?'

'Open your mind to it, kid. That's all I'd say to you. Imagine where I could send you. There's no end to the possibilities. But at the same time, don't be ridiculous. I mean, I get fellas looking at me, in all seriousness, and asking for the control of their thoughts. And I have to tell them straight, Ralph. Behave, I say. Get real.'

Ralph seems downhearted.

'But look,' says the genie, 'let's see if we can't rustle something up.'

The genie sketches a fresh design. He rethinks Ralph Coughlan. The new Ralph will have enough salt in him to meet a crisis head on. The new Ralph will parade the intimate streets with a sense of vigour and purpose. The lease on a new store will be arranged. It will be an elegant space in one of the nice laneways off the Mall, with Deco-style frontage. It will be high-end, without a brass monocular in sight, and handsome Ralph will tool around town in a low-slung Mercedes. Almost always as he rides he will get the run of the lights.

'All possible, Ralph,' says the genie, 'with just a wish or two. You see, one thing leads to another. This is how it works out. You make your fortune, then your fortune will make you.'

He paints a beautiful picture, this genie, but Ralph has had enough.

'No,' he says. 'We're going in the wrong direction here. As it happens, I've no great interest in material wealth.'

'Don't be distracted by the surface details,' says the genie. 'Surface is surface. All I'm asking you to do is to live intelligently.'

'What's that supposed to mean?'

'The only way to live a life elegantly, Ralph, is to live it with intelligence. And if you'd just use what you've already got, there is no reason why you can't do that. I can't tell you what to wish for. But I can tell you that each and all of us have boundless possibilities and if you know where to look, if you know where to search, if you reach deep within yourself and…'

'Genie?' Ralph interrupts. 'If you don't mind me saying, this is all getting a bit Whitney Houston.'

'Change or perish, Ralph.'

'Now what's that mean?'

'It means you have two choices.'

'Oh yeah?'

'Cluckety cluck. Try your luck.'

'You're… who the fuck are you?'

'Eat the world up, Ralph. Make a meal out of the place. Stop hiding in a junk shop down a filthy fucking quay. Get on with it! And name for me your second wish, please.'

Ralph pales.

'Is this about my wife?' he says.

The genie sighs, and throws his hands up. Why is he always given the fuckwits? Ralph Coughlan comes out from behind the counter and stalks the floor.

'I have you now,' he says. 'I have you now! And you know what, genie? You're absolutely spot on! That bitch is the bane of my life!

She's ground me down! So okay, fine, right, let's do it. I wish that I...'

'Ralph? Oh, Ralph. I really didn't take you for that type of client.'

'But you've brought it all home to me!' says Ralph, 'Jesus, do I ever need to have that weapon out of my life!'

The genie shrugs and takes a seat. He has heard it all before.

'She's sat on the couch above in Luke's Cross,' says Ralph, 'and the whole thing has her fucking mangled. If I hear another word about ovaries! And she isn't going to go anywhere, is she? Unless you can actually overdose on Chocolate Hobnobs, she isn't going to go anywhere, is she? So can you do anything for me there, genie? Can you do anything about that situation?'

'You're being sentimental, Ralph.'

'How so?'

'You're asking me to send you back. You want it to be all fluffy and lovely again, you want to turn the clock back.'

To when they'd walk on the long evenings to the Esso across from the brewery. They'd buy Cornettos: mint and pistachio for her, original flavour for him. They'd walk by the river, feeling pretty jaunty, because you're self-important with it when you're young, you carry it like a small dog carries a stick. She says, I hear there's going to be a heat wave. Yeah right, Brid. The windows of flats are left open and people play records—dub reggae, all the crooked-smiling dopeheads with their elbows on the sills—and the angles of the rooftops lean in on you. They make plans. They cross the shaky bridge and go up to one of the pubs in Sunday's Well. She gets amorous with a couple of drinks in her. The walk back home can be eventful and when you come outside, in the night-time, it's like you spiral, you spin out, and your lungs fill up with the cold-starred air. She says, do an Elvis, and he curls his lip and does the thing:

'Aw-haw-huh.'

'Okay,' says Ralph. 'Fine. You got me. I wish I could go back to that place. Can you send me back there?'

'You just been.'

The streets are thinning out. The traffic has started to bolt free of itself, atom by atom. Shadows slide down from the rooftops.

'You've one left, Ralph.'

'I'd just like an outstanding day. Alright? How about one out-standing day for me? And no fucking about. I wish, genie, for an outstanding day.'

The genie smiles.

'I'll do that for you now,' he says. 'Take it easy, killer.'

He clicks his fingers and is gone. He has given Ralph what's left of a dreary Tuesday in March. Ralph douses the bad lamp and drags a sweeping brush across the floor. Tomorrow might bring nostalgic people or at least somebody with an open-minded attitude to monoculars. He locks up and walks with squared shoulders down the street. He nods to the white-haired old dude pulling the shutters on the second-hand bookstore.

'How's business, Ralph?'

'Rockin' altogether. I'm beating 'em back with my bare hands.'

He steps into the corner shop and gets down on the floor and unplugs the chicken. He looks at the woman behind the counter and he says:

'I hear this asshole again, he goes in the river.'

He cuts across town to catch a number eight. He has it timed perfect. Just as he reaches Eason's, an eight pulls up. He pays for his ticket and goes upstairs. He takes a seat at the front, top right, over-head the driver. He'll be in at twenty past six for the tea. If there is any kind of God at all, it won't be the Shepherd's Pie. He wonders if he should try a few notes. Or give it an hour? The bus takes off and crosses the bridge and revs itself up to ascend into the northside... Oh where are the angels? Where are the trumpets? But all we've got is the teatime traffic, and the grey stone hills of the place, homicidal, and a deranged gull flies low over the water, then wheels away downriver for Little Island, Haulbowline, and points south.

There Are Little Kingdoms

It was deadening winter, one of those feeble afternoons with coal smoke for light, but I found myself in reliably cheerful form. I floated above it all, pleasantly distanced, though the streets were as dumb-witted as always that day, and the talkshops were a babble of pleas and rage and love declared, of all things, love sent out to Ukraine and Chad. It was midweek, and grimly the women stormed the veg stalls, and the traffic groaned, sulked, convulsed itself, and the face of the town was pinched with ill-ease. I had a song in my throat, a twinkle in my eye, a flower in my buttonhole. If I'd had a cane, I would have twirled it, unquestionably.

I passed down Dorset Street. I looked across to the launderette. I make a point always of looking into the launderettes. I like the steamy domesticity. I like to watch the bare fleshy arms as they fold and stack, load and unload, the busyness of it, like a Soviet film of the workers at toil. I find it quite comical, and also heartbreaking. Have the misfortunes no washing machines themselves, I worry? Living in old flats, I suppose, with shared hoovers beneath the stairs, and the smell of fried onions in the hallway, and the awful things you'd rather not hear late at night... turn up the television, will you, for Jesus' sake, is that a shriek or a creaking door?

And there he was, by the launderette window. Smoking a fag, if you don't mind. Even though I was on the other side of the street, I couldn't mistake him, he was not one you'd easily mistake. Steel-wire for hair, a small tight mushroom-shaped cloud of it, and he was wizened beyond his years, owlish, with the bones of the face arranged in a hasty symmetry that didn't quite take, and a torso too short for his long legs, heron's legs, and he was pigeon-chested, poetical, sad-faced.

I walked on, and I felt the cold rise into myself from the deep stone centre of the town. I quickened my pace. I was too scared to look back. I knew that he'd seen me too, and I knew that he would flee, that he would have no choice but to flee. He was one of my oldest and most argued with friends. He had been dead for six years.

I didn't stop until I reached the river. The banks of the river were peopled with the foul and forgotten of the town, skin-poppers and jaw-chewers, hanging onto their ratty dogs for dear life, eating sausage rolls out of the Centra, wearing thin nylon clothes against the seep of the evil-smelling air. The river light was jaunty, blue-green, it softened and prettified as best as it could. I sat on a bench and sucked down some long, deep breaths. If I had been able to speak, the words would have been devil words, spat with a sibilant hiss, all consonants and hate. Drab office workers in Dunnes suits chomped baguettes. People scurried, with their heads down. People muttered; people moaned. I tried to train my thoughts into logical arrangements but they tossed and broke free. I heard the oompah and swirls of circus music, my thoughts swung through the air like tiny acrobats, flung each other into the big tent's canvas maw, missed the catch, fell to the net.

I was in poor shape, but slowly the water started to work on me, calmed me, allowed me to corral the acrobats and put names to them. A car wreck, in winter, in the middle of the night, that had done for him, and there is no coming back from the likes of that, or so you would think. The road had led to Oranmore.

I tried my feet, and one went hesitantly in front of the other, and they sent me in the direction of Bus Áras. I decided there was nothing for it but to take a bus to the hills and to hide out for a while there, with the gentle people. I walked, a troubled man, in the chalk-stripe suit and the cheeky bowler, and this is where it got good. A barrier had been placed across the river's walkway and there was a sign tacked up. It read:

NO PEDESTRIAN ACCESS BEYOND THIS POINT

Fine, okay, so I crossed the road, but the throughway on Eden Quay was blocked too, with the same sign repeated, and I thought, waterworks, gasworks, cables, men in day-glo jackets, I'll cut up and around, but there was no access from Abbey Street, or from Store Street, everywhere the same sign had been erected: Bus Áras was a no-go zone. I saw a man in the uniform of the State, and he had sympathetic eyes, so I approached and questioned him.

'I am sorry, sir,' he said. 'There are no buses from here today. There are no buses in or out.'

I stood before him, horrified, and not because of the transport situation, which at the best of times wasn't great, but because this man in the uniform was undeniably Harry Carolan, a.k.a. Harry Cakes, the bread-and-fancies man of my childhood. The van would be around every day at half three, set your watch by it, loaves of white and loaves of brown, fresh baked, and ring doughnuts and jammy doughnuts and sticky buns too. The creased kind folds of his face, the happy downturned mouth, eyes that in a more innocent era we'd have described as 'dancing'. Éclairs! Fresh-cream swiss rolls! All the soda bread you could eat, until 1983, when Harry Cakes had dropped down dead in his shoes.

I went through the town like a flurry of dirty snow. This is a good one, I said to myself, oh this is a prize-taker. Now the faces of the streets seemed no different. It was the same bleary democracy as before. Some of us mad, some in love, some very tired, and all of us, it seemed, resigned to our humdrum affairs. People rearranged their shopping bags so as to balance the weight. Motorists tamped down their dull fury as best as they could. A busking trumpeter played 'Spanish Harlem'. I took on a sudden notion. I thought: might a bowl of soup not in some fundamental way sort me out?

There was a café nearby, on Denmark Street. I would not call it a stylish operation. It was a tight cramped space, with a small scattering of tables, greasy ketchup holders, wipeable plastic table cloths in a check pattern, Larry Gogan doing the just-a-minute quiz on a crackling radio, and I took a seat, composed myself, and considered the menu. It was written in a language I had no knowledge of. The slanted graphics of the lettering were a puzzle to me, the numerals were alien, I couldn't even tell if I was holding the thing the right way up. No matter, I thought, sure all I'm after is a drop of soup, and I clicked my fingers to summon the waiter.

You'd swear I'd asked him to take out his eyes and put them on a plate for me. The face on him, and he slugging across the floor, a big bruiser from the country.

'What's the soup, captain?' I asked.

'Carrot and coriander,' he said, flatly, as though the vocal chords were held with pliers. He seemed to grudge me the very words, and he did so in a midwestern accent and as always, this drew me in.

I considered the man. A flatiron face, hot with angry energies, mean thin mouth, aggravation in the oyster-grey eyes, and a challenging set to the jaw, anticipating conflict, which I had no intention of providing. I looked at him, wordlessly—you'll understand that by now I was somewhat adrift, as regards the emotions—and the café was on pause around us, and he grew impatient.

'Do you want the soup or what?' he said, almost hissed it, and it was at this point he clarified for me, I made out the childhood face in back of the adult's.

'It's Thomas, isn't it? Thomas Cremins?'

Sealight came into the oyster-grey, he gleamed with recognition, and it put the tiniest amount of happiness in his face—even this was enough to put some innocence back, too, and thus youth. He clarified still further: detail came back for me. He'd been one of those gaunt kids, bootlace thin and more than averagely miserable, a slime of dried snot on the sleeve of his school jumper. I remembered him on the bus home each day, waiting for someone braver to make the first move at hooliganism. A sheep, a follower, no doubt dull-minded, but somehow I remembered kindness in him, too. He said:

'Fitz?'

We talked, awkwardly but warmly, and with each sentence my own accent became more midwestern, and his circumstances came back to me. I remembered the small house, on a greystone terrace, near the barracks. Sometimes, after school, I would have been in there for biscuits and video games, and I remembered his sister, too, older and blousy, occasional fodder of forlorn fantasies, and of course there was his younger brother, younger than me but... ah.

Alan Cremins had been killed, hadn't he? Of course, it all came back. It had been one of these epochal childhood deaths some of us have the great excitement to encounter. He was caught in an April thunderstorm, fishing at Plassey, and he took shelter in a tower there and was struck by lightning. I remember the shine of fear on us all, for weeks after. Hadn't we all been fishing at Plassey, at some point or other, and hadn't we all seen the weather that day, it could have been each and any of us. It was about this same time I noticed girls. I liked big healthy girls with well-scrubbed faces. We had any amount of them in the midwest.

Should I mention it?

'I remember,' I said. 'Oh God, Thomas, I remember the time with Alan. When he, you know ...'

'Al?' he smiled. 'You remember Al?'

'Of course,' I said, though in truth it was vague. I remembered a slip of a child, a pale face, hadn't he, blue-veined I think, one of those cold-looking young fellas.

'Sure isn't he inside,' beamed Thomas, and he called out:

'Al! Come here I want you!'

Alan Cremins, in chef pants and a sweat-drenched tee-shirt, with a tureen's ladle in his hand, stepped through the swing doors of the kitchen and he smiled at me, a somewhat foxed smile.

'Fitz?' he said.

Grotesque! Horrible! A child's head on a full-grown man's body! I legged it. What else could I do? Away into the winter streets, these malignant streets, and I raved somewhat at the falling skies: you couldn't but forgive me for that.

By and by, anger overtook my despair. Frankly, I'd had enough of this messing for one day. I raised the collars of my jacket and dug my hands into the pockets of my trousers. I hunched my shoulders against the knifing wind. The sky was heavy with snow, and it began to fall, and each drop had taken on the stain of the town before it hit the pavement. Chestnut sellers huddled inside their ancient greatcoats. Beggars whittled the dampness off sticks to keep the barrel fires stoked. The talkshops sang in dissonant voices. Tyres squealed angrily in the slush. Black dogs roamed in packs. We were all of us in the town bitten with cold, whipped by the wind, utterly ravaged by this mean winter, but we stomped along, regardless, like one of those marvellously tragic Russian armies one reads about.

Of course, yes. The obvious explanation did present itself, and as I slipped along the streets, heading north out of town, I considered it. If the dead were all around me, was it conceivable that I myself had joined their legion ranks? Was this heaven or hell on the North Circular Road? A ludicrous idea, clearly—I was in far too much pain not to be alive. I soldiered on. I began to wind my way slowly westwards and the streets quietened of commerce and became small terrace streets, and toothless crones huddled in the sad grogshops, and from somewhere there was the scrape of a plaintive fiddle. A man with a walrus moustache came along, all purposeful, and he passed a handbill to me. It announced a public meeting the Saturday coming: Larkin was the promised speaker, his topic predictably dreary.

I made it to the park, and it was desolate, with nobody at all to be seen, and it calmed me to walk there. I came across some of the park's tame deer. They were huddled behind a windbreak of trees, and I stopped to watch them. The tough-skinned bucks seemed comfortable enough in the extreme weather, but the does and the fawns had to work hard at it—there were rolling shudders of effort along their flanks as they took down the cold air, and the display of this was a symptom of glorious life, and my heart rose.

Fawns! I was clearly in a highly emotional state, and I thought it best to make a move for home. Jesus' sake, Fitzy, I said, come on out of it, will you, before they arrive with the nets.

I went into the northwestern suburbs of the town, the patch that I had made my home, and I allowed no stray thoughts. By sheer force of will, I would put the events of the afternoon behind me. I made it at last to my quiet, residential street in my quiet, residential suburb. I rent there the ground floor of an ageing semi, and the situation I find ideal. I have a sitting room, a lounge, a neat, single man's bedroom, and a pleasant, light kitchen from which French doors open to a small, oblong garden, and to this I have sole access. I turned the key and stepped inside. I brushed the dirty snow from my shoulders, and I allowed the weight of the day to slide from me with the chalkstripe jacket. I blew on my hands to warm them. I went through to the kitchen area and drank a glass of water. I then pulled open the French doors and stepped outside.

I stepped into glorious summer. The fruit trees were full in bloom, and it was the dense languor of July heat, unmistakable, and I unfolded my striped deckchair and sat back in it. The transistor was by my feet and I turned it on for the gentle strings, for the swoons and lulls of the afternoon concert. I removed my galoshes and my shoes and stockings, and I stretched ten pale toes on the white-hot concrete of the patio. I unfolded my handkerchief and tied it about my head. I turned up the sleeves of my shirt, and opened the top three pearl buttons to reveal an amount of scrawny chest. I listened: to the soft stir of the notes, and the trills and scratchings of insect life all around, and the efficient buzzing of the hedge strimmers, and the children of the vicinity at play. They played crankily in the sun, and it was my experience that the hot days could make the children come over rather evil-eyed and scary, beyond mere mischief, and sometimes on the warm nights they lurked till all hours around the streets, they hid from me in the shadows, and played unpleasant tricks, startling me out of my skin as I walked home from the off-licence.

Drinks were all I was required to provide for myself. Since I had begun this lease, I found that the shelves daily replenished themselves. Nothing fancy, but sufficient: fresh fruit and veg, wholemeal breads, small rations of lean meat and tinned fish, rice and pasta, tubs of stir-in sauce, leaf tea, occasionally some chocolate for a treat. I had a small money tin in the kitchen, and each time I opened it, it contained precisely eight euro and ninety-nine cent, which was the cost of a drinkable rioja at the nearby branch of Bargain Booze. Utilities didn't seem to be an issue—no bills arrived. In fact, there was no mail from anywhere, ever.

The phone, however, was another matter. Sometimes, it seemed as if the thing never stopped, and it rang now, and I sighed deeply in my deckchair, and I lifted my ageless limbs. I went inside to it—summoned! The power of the little fucker.

'Uphi uBen?' said the voice. 'Le yindawo la wafa khona?'

'I'm sorry,' I replied, wearily. 'I have no idea what you're talking about. Didn't get a word.'

'Ngifanele ukukhuluma naye.'

'No,' I said. 'Not getting this at all. Thank you.'

I hung up, and waited, for the calls always came in threes, and sure enough, it immediately rang again.

'Chce rozmawiac z Maria! Musze powiedziec jej, ze ja kocham!'

'Please!' I said. 'Don't you speak any English at all?'

'For sure,' he said, and hung up.

The third call was promptly put through.

'An bhfuil Tadgh ann? An bhfaca tú Tadhg?'

'I don't know any Tadhgs!' I cried. 'I haven't seen any Tadhgs!'

I'd complained several times to the Exchange, for all the good it had done me, but I thought I may as well try again. I dialled the three-digit number and was quickly connected to a faceless agent. The Exchange was part of the apparatus of the State that seemed to be a law onto itself. I gave my name and my citizen tag-number.

'I'm getting the calls again,' I said. 'It's been a bad week, it's been practically every day this week and sometimes at night, too. Can you imagine what this is doing to my nerves? There's been no improvement at all. You promised it would improve!'

'Who promised, sir?'

'One of your agents.'

'Which agent, sir?'

'How would I know? I wasn't given the agent i.d., was I?'

'No you were not, sir. We are hardly permitted to enter into personal terms with citizens of the State. It would be untoward, sir. This *is* the Exchange, sir.'

'Well how can I tell if…'

'Please hold.'

A maudlin rendition of 'Spanish Harlem', on trumpet, and I whistled along, miserably. I had fallen into melancholy—the drab old routine of these days can get to a soul. But I was determined not to hang up. They expect you to hang up, you see, and in this way, they can proceed, they can get away with their thoughtlessness. The music faded out, and I was given a series of fresh options.

'If you wish to hear details of the Exchange's new evening call rates, please press one.'

I threw my eyes to the heavens.

'If you would like a top-up for your free-go, anywhere-anytime service, please press two.'

I refused to carry one of those infernal contraptions.

'If you wish to discuss employment opportunities at the Exchange, and to hear details of our screening arrangements, and of our physical and mental requirements for operatives, voice engineers and full-blown agents, please press three.'

I'd rather work in the sewers.

'If you seek an answer to the sense of vagueness that surrounds your existence like a fine mist, please press four.'

I pressed four. A happy voice exploded in my ear. It was the voice of heartiness. It was the voice of a resort manager at a mid-priced beach destination. It was a kind of stage Australian.

'Watcha!' it said. 'Feelin' kinda grooky, mate? What ya wanna do, ya wanna go down yar garden, ya wanna go down them fruit trees, and ya wanna find the ladder that's hidden there, right? Then what do ya do? YA BLOODY WELL CLIMB IT!!!'

The phone cut out—dead air. I proceeded directly to the garden. I put on a pair of plimsolls. I removed the handkerchief from my head. I walked down to the dense, summer tangle of fruit trees. I pulled back the hanging vines, parted the thick curtains of growth, and I could see nothing, at first, but then my eyes adjusted to the dappled half-light and I made out a dull, golden gleam, and yes, it was a ladder. I pushed my way through, thorns snagging on my trousers, and I began to climb. Slowly, painfully, I ascended through the thick foliage and I came to the treetops, and a view of my suburb, its neat hedges and mossy slate rooftops, and I climbed on, and I went into the white clouds and I climbed still higher, and the ladder rose up against rocky outcrops. I found that I was climbing past the blinding limestone of a cliff-face, and at last I got to the top, and

I hauled myself up onto the salty, springy turf.

I walked. The marine breeze was pleasant, at first, after my sweaty efforts, but soon it started to chill me. It was a bright but blowy spring day, and the first of the cliff-top flowers were starting to appear: the tormentil, the early orchids, the bird's foot trefoil. A milky white sea lapped below, it had latent aggression in it, and I looked down the stretch of the coastline and oh, I don't know, it may have been Howth, or Bray, or one of these places. There was nobody around. Black-headed terns battled with the wind and rose up on it, they let it turn and throw them: sheer play. I walked, and I concentrated on clearing my mind. I wanted to white out now. I wanted to leave all of it behind me again.

Yes I walked, I walked into the breeze, and after a time I came to one of those mounted telescopes, the kind that you always get at the seaside. I searched in my pocket, found a half-crown, inserted it, and the block slid away on the eyepiece and I looked through. There appeared to be a problem with the telescope—it was locked in place, it wouldn't swivel and allow me to scan the water, the shore, the sky. It was locked onto a small circle of grey shingle, just by the water's edge, and I saw that it was a cold and damp day down there. It was winter by the tide-line, it was springtime on the cliffs.

I kept looking, and she appeared. She crouched on her heels and looked out over the water. She wore a long coat, belted, and a wool scarf about her throat. It wasn't a close-up view but even so, I could see that age had gone on her. I could see the slump of adult weariness. The view was in black and white, flickering, it was old footage, a silent movie, and I knew that the moment down there had passed, too, and that she herself was long gone now. If I was to find her again, it would be pure chance, a random call coming through the Exchange. And I would try to explain, I would. I'd try to tell her why it had happened the way that it did, but my words would sink beneath the waves, where shock-bright colours surprise the gloom: the anemones and starfish and deadman's fingers, the clam and the barnacle, the brittlestar.

The eyepiece blacked out and I walked back the way that I came. I descended the ladder to an autumn garden. Russets and golds and a bled, cool sky: turtleneck weather. My favourite time, the season of loss and devotion.

Nights At The Gin Palace

Wifeless ten years, at large in the ancient house, prey to odd shudders in the small hours, Freddie Bliss had more or less given up on the idea of sleep. Subsequently he had gone a little daft. But sleep? No. He had no time for it anymore. Life is precious—grab as much of it as you can. This was the Freddie Bliss philosophy.

'They've stopped the night outside High Hesket,' said his daughter, Angelica, a large peach-skinned woman in her flailing forties. 'They've bunked up at a Roadsleeper and they'll be heading here first thing. There's a crew of twelve. There are two trucks for equipment. They want to know if there are any characters among the builders.'

'What builders?'

'Well, this is the problem, isn't it? I wonder is it too late to get Joe up? He's larger than life, Joe. But there's the question of his tags, isn't there?'

'His what?'

'TAGS! His probation. Though they might make an exception for TV.'

'Jailbird, is he? Another one, Angel?'

'Miscarriage of justice,' she said, and with a noiseless swivel of her powerful shoulders she swung the giant mallet hammer at an internal wall.

'That bitch was psychotic! Joe acted purely in self-defence. Of course he had previous, I grant you.'

Freddie Bliss mouthed a soft note of sympathy, and he continued his search for drink.

'It's an outrage, Daddy, what these old bastards in the courts get away with. Whoremasters, the lot of them!'

'What's he inside for?'

'Are you listening to a single word? Turn your ears on! I said PROBATION! I said MISCARRIAGE OF JUSTICE!'

'Oh!' said Freddie Bliss. 'You needn't tell me! I lost all faith in the legal system in 1974, Angel. Remember the business with the gypsies? Remember whose side the courts took? Well! Never again, I said. Never again will I submit to those dogs.'

Angelica put down the mallet hammer, wiped her brow, and paced the faded linoleum of the kitchen floor. She was in a condition of high wrath but she stopped, suddenly, and stared off into space—she had been arrested by gentle thoughts. She closed her eyes, and held her head at a respectful incline. She slid a stockinged toe up her calf to attend an itch.

'Joe,' she whispered, 'is a gentle, oh a gentle man! He is so loving, Daddy, and kind. It's the small things that he does, the tiny things! They make the man. I can actually say that I consider myself a very, very lucky woman.'

'I'm delighted for you, dear. It's time you had some luck. I'm afraid you've rather been through the wringer.'

Dapper Bliss rummaged among the bottles for something to stiffen the coffee. Angelica wasn't a terrific one for sleep either, and now the pair of them were often to be found, late on, arranging a brew, as the night birds fluted outside, and the old shale earth sent up its black breaths. She had come home, at last, to settle. The plan was to turn the place into a guesthouse. But no, not a guesthouse. If he said guesthouse, she flew into a rage.

'I'm not talking a bloody B&B! I'm talking A BOUTIQUE FUCK-ING HOTEL!'

The Bliss place was big enough, certainly, and it had bags of character. The countryside was bleak but impressive: fells and stone hills and sudden gorges. Angelica felt there were opportunities with walkers, dreamers, romantic types. She admitted there was work to be done. The house had animals in its walls. It had structural concerns. There was the wafting presence of the Bliss ancestral dead.

From an exotic assortment of spirits, Freddie considered something green and conceivably... Venezuelan? He held the bottle against the window and moonlight made lurid the unreal green of its liquor. Well, one took one's chances.

'I must say,' he said, with a relaxed grin. 'I'm very much looking forward to the guided badger walks.'

'Nothing is decided on badgers,' she held up a warning finger.

'But it'll be a unique attraction,' he argued. 'Badger sightings are terribly rare. And I happen to know just the spot. I'll tell you now, Angel—I can all but guarantee badgers. Of course, these will be nocturnal events, obviously, but that just adds to the fun of it. Nighttime expeditions! A cloak of darkness!'

Freddie Bliss was about to go with the Venezuelan when he spotted half a bottle of decent-looking Spanish brandy at the back of the press. This was a definite result. He waved the dusty treasure at his daughter and set free a suave smile.

'Come, my darling,' he said. 'The night is young.'

Angelica narrowed her eyes. She retained—despite it all—a good posture. She wore light fabrics in bright colours. She had a fondness for ethnic trousers, loosely worn, and these did not flatter. She had some handsomeness still but it was turning into something else. She had moved from city to city, and from town to town, propelled by a talent for hopeless optimism.

'I'm warning you, Dad,' she said. 'What I've told you about Joe is in the strictest confidence. He'd be livid if he thought every old sod knew his difficulties.'

'Where do you find these blokes, Angel? Pubs?'

'Don't be ridiculous.'

'Seedy night-spots?'

'Shut up! What do think I am? Some kind of tart?'

'Well where did you meet him?'

'We met on the Internet.'

'I see,' said Freddie Bliss, assuming some kind of motorway junction.

The warmth in the air was still and oily feeling. Soon the lake would turn stagnant and rank. The yellow flowers of the gorse would dry out and become a nose-tickling dust. That was the first sign of the year turning.

'I've been wondering…' she said.

She picked up the mallet again and swung it thoughtfully to test its heft.

'I've been wondering if maybe we should… knock through some more? We've started so we'll finish, kind of a thing.'

'More, sweet? I'd be worried about draughts.'

Three internal walls had already come down. All was rubble and wreck. For weeks, Angelica had stomped around in brown padded boots like builders wear, in a facemask, wielding the mallet, with her cheeks a flushed red against the whiteness of plaster and dust. A space the size of a football pitch had been cleared out downstairs. She now spent much of the evenings crawling around with a chalk, marking down where the new divisions would go.

'You mean,' said Freddie, 'that now we put up new walls?'

'Perhaps just screens,' she said.

'Like Japanese?'

'Precisely, Dad. Lacquered.'

'Lovely.'

'I'm thinking fin de siecle. I want an opulent feel. Decadent!'

'Like a knocking shop?' said Freddie Bliss.

'More opium den,' she said.

The curriculum vitae of Angelica Bliss:

She went first to art school in Leeds, where she discovered no aptitude for creativity, but fell happily pregnant by her free-drawing instructor, Kim, who was kind enough to drive her to Halifax for the abortion, and with a Yorkshireman's swarthy panache offered to go halves on the cost. Then she took up archaeology at Liverpool, and talked excitedly for two years of Picts, Celts, and Roman walls, and she was neck-deep in mud on digs in North Wales, and the dig supervisor, Frank, vowed to leave his wife of thirty years for her, and there was a dreadful scene in a lay-by outside Wrexham: midnight, winter, early eighties. She had enough of learning then, thank you very much, and with a loan from her parents opened a candle store in Stoke-on-Trent. From there, she progressed to a transcendence workshop in Inverness, then a market stall in Camden Town, then a lost weekend in Murcia that lasted five years, then a period of intense political activism on behalf of the Turks in Dortmund, then a marriage of one year to a financial services executive in Kent, then a squat strewn with needle-thin junkies in Coventry, and finally a dull job at a call centre in Manchester. She had long since gone through her inheritance: all that was left was the house. She now stood in the middle of the house, late on a summer's night, with the mallet hammer in her hands.

'What we also need to think about,' she said, 'is the breakfast menu. Traditional? Kippers?'

She swung the mallet. She took out a doorframe. There had as yet been little discussion about marketing. Angelica believed that once the camera crew had been, and once the programme aired, their name would be out there, and it would spread, and the business would make itself. She held the firm belief, always, that if your name was Bliss, then the stars were helpfully arrayed. Significantly, this had not proved the case for previous generations.

'Actually,' she said, throwing the hammer aside. 'We really need to start getting some ideas down. They'll be here for seven. Sharp!'

'I've had a shave,' said Freddie Bliss. 'And I've given quite a bit of thought to what I'd like to say.'

'What you mean, like to say?'

'To camera.'

'This isn't about you! This is a renovation show.'

'Fly on the wall, you said?'

'Oh you know the type of thing, Dad. We're battling against the odds. We're setting up a new business. This is a story about life changes and DIY. The last-minute madness of the renovation. The drama of the first paying guests.'

'You mean there's a booking?'

'Oh shut up! We'll go out on the eight o'clock slot. The eating-your-supper slot. All we've got to worry about is keeping up with the business as it arrives.'

The scullery ceiling caved in. Angelica shrugged heroically.

'I rather thought,' said Freddie Bliss, 'that I'd talk about… courage.'

'Oh dear Christ!'

'I've never had any. Now you certainly do, Angel. You're a tremendously brave girl.'

'You're background colour! You can say hello and look whiskery and that's it!'

'I'm worried about the lights. Will there be lots? Will there be… kliegs? If there are going to be kliegs, I'd better have a word.'

They repaired to what was left of the dining room. It was a house of scurrying and of rising damp. Angelica remained confident they would be open for business in three weeks. Freddie couldn't see it, unless they were to put the guests on beds of straw. But he was no longer a man to fret. He was, in the calmness of his age, a great believer in doing things right: after dinner, you have some more drinks.

He placed the bottle on the table with a triumphant flourish and then sniffed at the air, sighed, and went to open the windows. Torpid and clammy, it was June, and the gorse on the low hills was an invitation to midges. The smoke from the candlelight would keep most of them at bay. He lit more, to be on the safe side. Angelica poured the coffee. Freddie added generous slugs of the cognac. It was a brand from the northern bit, something unpronounceable with lots of Xs and Ks, and it had a badly drawn bull for a graphic.

'This should do the business, Angel,' he said, as though predicting a safe landing in hazardous conditions. 'Carajillos, isn't it? Civilised.'

'If we must,' said Angelica.

'No gun to your head, dear. You mustn't always scold so.'

'I'm not scolding.'

'It's your tone. It's a scolding tone.'

It was falling so quickly into the patterns of a marriage. Some wind got up and the old house groaned and trembled. If the house ever stopped groaning and trembling, it would be time to worry. There were presences in the house, he was sure, but mostly benign. His Uncle Jack for one. Poor Jack! Jack was always going to be a man for the unquiet grave.

'So what colour's this one? What colour's Joe?'

'Oh! You're unbelievable! You realise, I suppose, that you can be arrested for that type of comment now? They won't care if you're eighty-five! Joe is an honest and kind and loving man, he's...'

'Relax, Angel, you'll give yourself blood pressure. He's Manchester, is he? Well, rough old spot, isn't it? I remember it must have been... '38? Yes, and I'm in a low bar in Ancoats. No, hang on, was it Huyton? Remember the rhyme? Huyton, Huyton, two dogs fightin'! No, Huyton's Liverpool. It was Manchester, it was Ancoats. Myself, Alec Whittle, Charlie Bamber, all that crowd. I dare say we've had a few. Ambrose Poll walks in, he says ...'

'Dad,' said Angelica. 'The last thing I need now is pub stories. You're stinking.'

'No, actually,' said Freddie. 'I've only had a couple.'

'You're stinking,' she said. 'You were stinking when I got back at two o'clock today—two o'clock, Daddy!—and you're stinking now.'

'Three or four, darling,' he said. 'That's all I've had.'

'Stinking. At your age!'

'Your mother was never a shrew. Your mother was a marvellous woman. Liked a drink. Wonderful with money. Knew her horses. And she ate very rarely.'

'You're a washed up old sot. I should put you in a facility.'

'You come up here!' he cried. 'You come up here with your bloodshot eyes! You bed the jailbird!'

She leapt to her feet and took the bottle by its neck.

'How dare you! You drove my mother to the grave and you won't be happy till you've me in t'same place! You go out of your mind! You lose the fucking plot! I mean that business with the headstones, Dad! The police called in? Community orders? At your age? You have disgraced this family's name! AGAIN! We are lower than muck now! People smirk, in the village, they do! When I pass? They smirk!'

'Angelica,' he said. '*Really.*'

Bliss family arguments boiled up quick and subsided as fast. They had a couple of sips, they took down a couple of breaths. They gathered themselves.

'Hillwalkers?' he said.

'That's our market.'

'Enormous gasping Germans in boots. Well, they're back, certainly. Like the swallows. They're all over the shop. They turn up here, you know? Bang on the door at all hours. They get lost. They say this direction is west, please? This direction is east? I say no wonder you lost the war. Can't find your way to Keswick? How do you expect to find Moscow? In the snow?'

'I'm headachey,' said Angelica.

'Blonde chaps. Healthy, yes, but tremendously dull, Germans. Don't you find? Headache, darling? Eat some pills.'

The drinks became more brandy than coffee. She drained hers and went to the window for air. It was an enormous, leaded window, like a church's, and she pushed it open as wide as it'd go, and climbed out for a turn about the unkempt gardens. It was a clear night and the sky was jewelled and the Plough was precisely where it should be at this late hour, indicating Carlisle. She had plans for a meditation space by the froggy pond. There would be dawn ceremonies. She had a loose white frock in mind. Also, she would relay the croquet lawn. There would be cream teas, served by pleasant local girls in crisp linen uniforms—that is the sort of thing that gets the foreigners gushing and ensures repeat business.

She fished the phone from her trouser pocket and texted some filth to Joe. He liked his filth, Joe. Perhaps it would be best if she didn't hire girls who were overly pleasant. As soon as he was untagged, Joe would move up, and they would set about building their new life together. She had at last found her soul mate. She had known from the very first moment, six weeks ago. She exhaled raw happiness into the night-time garden. She danced back to the dining room for another drink or two.

Freddie Bliss had gone into reminiscence.

'Lucia! Oh, she hated a snob. Marvellous throat, so sleek, like a swan! You've taken after my lot, more's the pity. Bad luck, darling! Nose of a Bliss, certainly. Bulgy. Like your Uncle Alex. He went mad, you know. Poor Alex. That was a terrible end for any man to suffer, not to say bizarre. The papers were full of it. But Lucia! What does she do? Drives off the bridge at Ennerdale! Thought she was taking a left for Moresby Parks. Half in the bag, of course.'

'You can convince yourself of anything, can't you?' said Angelica, pouring.

'It was an accident, Angel! Lucia was in tremendous form that morning. She was right as rain.'

'Dad? I think it's time you thought about beddie-byes, no?'

'Oh no,' said Freddie. 'It's only half past two, dear. And may I apologise, again, for dinner being a shade late to table? It's the dratted oven. Again! I'll have to have a man over. Must be the fan. But no, dear, really, I sleep very little these days.'

A night bird's call, it carried sadness to the room, and also the silver of hypochondria.

'I think I've a fever coming up,' said Angelica, hand to brow. 'It's the stress of the business. We need to sort out bedding, cutlery, flowers! We need to think about the painting and the plastering. There's the question of staff. There are slates on the roof want replacing. Are you quite sure about the bank?'

'Afraid so, darling. Chap went so far as to say it was one of the worst credit ratings ever recorded in the Northwest. I said, how dare you!'

The night murmured on, regardless. The night went about its clammy business. He watched Angelica with great interest. There wasn't so much fun in the old thing anymore. Ah but when she was tiny! Some days, Lucia would take to the bed with one of her spells— Lucia got weak and pale and ranted sometimes—and Freddie would be put in charge of the baby. Those days were tremendous. He'd wheel her down the village in the pram. He remembered autumn weather, equinoctal gales. Hold on to your hair! And pushing the pram along, whistling, and the pram was a shield against the world. He'd take her down The Beekeepers in the afternoons, have a couple of swift ones. A malty ale, lovely, a scan of the paper, and her baby fists jabbing at the dust motes. It was late in the fifties. He was calming.

'I've got it!' she cried. 'What if we called it 'The Old Rectory'?'

'Of course!' said Freddie. 'Because it was a rectory! Brilliant, Angel. Funny how things work out, eh? The likes of us? In a house of God? Lucia found it a frightfully glum notion. Oh Freddie, she said, a rectory? How dour! Uncle Jack wangled something with the Church. Place hadn't been used in years. Parishes amalgamate, don't they? There seemed to be no objection to me getting the keys. The deeds were another trick but there was little beyond Lucia. So I do actually have the deeds, dear, yes.'

'A little sleep, Dad, don't you think? Just for a while? Before the crew gets in.'

The house's ragged orchestra struck up. Freddie heard it always as a small-town ensemble. He heard the wounded strings. He saw the bald elbows of the violinist's rented dress suit. He saw the shiny pate of the third-rate conductor, consigned to the provinces after some murky scandal.

'I remember the first night here. We ran around opening windows. We lifted the covers off the furniture. The birds, Freddie, she said, all the birds! I said yes, darling, there are very many birds, and there were, they were flying all over the bloody house—holes in the roof, hadn't we?—and I opened some more of the wine. We didn't at that point have any idea about the presences. The guests will have to get used. Jack himself generally keeps to the back rooms. I have no great trouble with Jack.'

'I don't believe any more,' said Angelica.

'You will again,' said Freddie. 'Of course I forget sometimes, at night, which is natural. I think she's gone to the loo. I shout out: Lucia! Hurry up, darling! You'll get your end! It's bloody freezing in there. Carpets rather than tiles, maybe?'

'I'm going to take my pulse,' said Angelica.

'Actually it's probably what put me off the dozing,' said Freddie. 'But of course there's always Italy, as well, isn't there? To be honest,

Angel, I don't talk about it much. Not a great distance from Bolzano, I think. Oh! Difficult. Think about something else, that's what I say.'

'One hundred and four!' said Angelica.

'I don't know about you, dear, but I'm about ready for another.'

The night progressed as the nights did. He talked of the trade in antiques among the long gone intimates of its northwestern scene. He talked of Charlie Bamber and Ambrose Poll. He confided the racetrack intrigue of the Skipton Fancy. He rescued the reputation of Freddie Bliss from the hammering it had taken in the infamous gypsy trial of '74. He grew agitated when he told of the snubbing his wife had received from some of the other ladies—so-called!—of the area. Alice Hemshaw? Snivelling old trout, with her pearls and her bony elbows, with her gums. He paced the floor, with a glass of ancient Madeira to hand.

'We were blow-ins,' he said. 'You never get over that. We were never churchy, of course, and that didn't help. Never played golf. Never sailed. We liked a drink. We liked a flutter. We had fun! Is that a crime? Well string me up and flay me!'

Outside, the tawnies were hunting. It was quickening June, and there was an urgency. It was almost four o'clock in the northern summer. The house had settled over its long years, it had hunkered down into the Cumbrian shale. To achieve great age requires constant negotiation, and all of the late night groans and creaks were no more than the wheedling of the dispute. But lately there was a new nervousness to the house's soundings. It had not reckoned on the return of a grown Angelica.

She went to the kitchen and booted the laptop and the *whoosh* and the *whumpf* as it took life was so familiar, a reassurance. She went to eBay and increased her bid for some ochre-coloured tiles reclaimed from the palace of a Carpathian count. She went to her usual chatroom and flirted a little with a reformed arsonist from the Black Country. He had been coming on fruity these past nights: she would have to dampen his ardour. She was spoken for. She checked her mail: nothing much. She took strangely, then: she was at once in the damp and green of anxiety.

In the dining room, Freddie Bliss stood by the bay window and spoke to the last of the night.

'The immediate concern was footwear,' he said. 'Boots, plain as. A stout pair of boots can save a man. And under the circumstances, we knew that, with the what-you-call-it coming… what do you call it? In winter? The shortest day? What do you call it?'

He turned to an empty room, and smiled.

'Ah,' he said. 'Never mind. I know! Solstice.'

He set to writing some notes. He still had a supply of the letter-head paper from Bliss Antiques, which had gone out of business in 1975. If the television people finished up early, Angelica might manage a trip to the village. Freddie didn't go so much now. He sent down notes instead. He wrote one for the video man.

'Please,' it said, 'nothing else with this Tom Hanks person,' and the name was twice underlined.

Angelica returned. She appeared to be having trouble breathing.

'You look gaunt, darling.'

'I've got NIGHT FEAR!' she cried.

She picked up the mallet and slapped at the wall. This was the wall that divided the pantry from the dining room. The plaster crumbled, willingly enough, but the brickwork was stubborn. Angelica was fagged out—she hadn't the strength for large-scale destruction at this hour. She was determined, however, to keep busy.

'This old rad,' she said, 'how long since we've had heat out of it?'

Freddie Bliss considered the rusty, leak-stained radiator and thought for a moment.

'The sixties?' he tried.

'Right,' said Angelica, and fetched the claw hammer.

Freddie Bliss made some fresh drinks. He always kept a little of the good stuff back for late on. The fizz of the tonic quieted by the dash of the gin. The glass clouding up as the limes cut in. Poetry, and Angelica, panting, attempted to wrench the rad from the wall. She got it part ways out, and then stopped.

'What's this?'

'What's what, Angel?'

She yanked up a clutch handbag, so old to be almost fashionable, its grey leather softened and cracked with age.

'Must be one of your mother's. It must have fallen down there. Show!'

She opened the bag and spread its contents on the dining-room table. Freddie Bliss was rapt with attention: he was half thinking there might be an old tenner forgotten. But it was mostly photographs, from the war years and before. Training at Carlisle. The weekend trips home before shipping out. Arm in arm in a pub, the pair of them shining with youth and love, in the autumn of 1942. There were a few of his letters home, those that had got through, with lines of neat Xs for kisses. There was the notification of dishonourable discharge from His Majesty's Forces.

'Why has she got all this here?'

'It's what she'd have hidden on me,' said Freddie Bliss.

'Why not just burn the stuff?'

'It's important,' he said, and he shrugged. 'But it doesn't matter now.'

It didn't matter. Enough time had passed. These were the remnants of another life, and he could look on that life as a stranger would. Angelica sobbed.

'Courage, dear,' he said.

'Courage!'

'I never had any,' he said. 'I think you've shown some, I really do. But not me. Ambrose Poll? Yes. Charlie Bamber? Charlie absolutely dripped with the stuff. But Freddie Bliss? No. I scampered!'

He moved through the woods. This was Italy, 1943. He had a flame of colour in his cheeks, and the ice had formed into a webbing between the black bones of the trees. The sun through the ice made a palatial blue light, and he winced. At each crack of the ice, he jumped from his skin. He had lost his coat. In the panic of his flight, everything had got thrown in the air. His old boots had split open. He felt the cold come in. His fingertips blackened with bite. There were moments he thought he had passed over. He had to fight hard to distinguish himself as a living thing, among the trees and the ice, beneath the sky. His vision started to blur. His fear went. He fell down in the snow. Smiling, he lifted his head from the ground. In the near distance, the whites and blues of winter were disturbed by a shape that had a smokiness to it, a dark shimmering, and he crawled to it and found that it was a horse. It had been slit along its belly and it lay dead in the snow but it had its heat still. He lay with it. He huddled as close to it as he could get. He scolded himself. He said you shan't, oh you can't, and then he did. He put his hands into the wound and dug them deep. He forced his arms in, past the elbows. The organ heat saved him but his mind became unseated. He became weightless, untethered. It was as if he had stepped off a plane.

He confronted the lifeless gin in his hand. The limes were no use. They were past their best and shrivelled quickly in the alcohol. They spoiled the drink with a sour green tinge. There would have to be a note for the grocer.

'We'd go down The Philly,' he said. 'Every single night, we'd be on the tiles. She insisted. We'd go down The Chophouse. She'd bloody well drag me! I'd whimper! I was rattling, Angel! I wasn't right for donkey's! But she'd say get this into you, sweetness. Chin up now!'

'We'll be thinking about breakfast,' said Angelica.

She had calmed again, but to a state of listlessness. She checked her phone.

'No word from Joe.'

'What about a walk, Angel?'

'If he's broken his tag bounds? If he's gone to Bolton? That's trouble, Dad, with a capital T.'

'Bolton! Frightful place. Full of low-lifes, always has been. What about a walk?

'A walk? Now? But it's still dark.'

'All the better,' he said.

It was one of the few nights of the northern year there would be no need for a jacket. He held himself beautifully as he walked. He was straight backed and steady as he moved. Nobody walks like Freddie Bliss any more. Angelica loped along beside him, breathless. From a high distance, if you looked back, the house had a jaunty air.

The east wing had an attractive lopsided feel, the gale-tormented west was grimly hanging on, and there were shades watching from the windows.

They walked over the rough ground. You'd twist an ankle if you didn't know it. They went by the pathway along the stretch of trees that led down to the lake. Time was passing. He stopped, suddenly, and put a finger to his lips. By the water, there was a blurred movement, the air and the darkness shifted, and she saw the black and white of them, the striped noses and beady red eyes, and then at once they were everywhere, they wrestled and flipped each other over, they tumbled and righted themselves. Angelica gripped her father's hand. Angelica held her breath. Cheerfully, with the air of an old familiar, Freddie Bliss addressed the badgers:

'Good morning!' he said.

Recovery had been learned. When young, she had taught him again the language of relish.

The Penguins

The shudders and jolts of an old jumbo, pulling back the hours. Across the Hudson Bay we sail and over the Labrador Sea. This is the part we call the feeding of the seals. We come down the aisles, in our frayed uniforms, with our smiles fixed as death's rictus, and their anxious heads swivel to us, and there are hoarse little barks of delight as we fling out the foil-covered trays. They pull back the foil, burn their fingertips, blow on their fingertips, and steam clouds rise to numb their tired faces. The steam clears to reveal the griddled flesh of what once was fowl, and the annihilated broccoli, and the Nagasaki carrots, and they make small brave noises; they begin.

The eternal question across the rows-of-three and the rows-of-six: isthisthechicken isthisthechicken isthisthe… chicken???

Personally speaking? I would touch nothing bar the salad.

At the top of the rows-of-three, left aisle, just across from my station, in the row with the extra leg room—it is our handsome gift to bestow—there is an elderly couple, bright-eyed with enthusiasm/medication.

'Tell you that right there looks to me like fresh snow,' he says.

'But it's nearly May already,' she says.

'Nothing surprises me about weather anymore,' he says.

The crushed democracy of the cheap seats—their knees are high and their eyes are hopeful. The piebald mountains rise and dip beneath, there are slopes of black ice and sharp crests and thin blue streams, then an expanse of turfy scrag a rich brown like chocolate.

In the top row-of-six:

The babymamma of a Lithuanian gangster.

A nervous African priest.

A pair of square-jaw corporates in casual flight wear.

A leathery Balkan ponce.

A sour-faced French hottie with the tiniest feet, who wrinkles her photoshop-perfect nose and looks across, irritated, to the row-of-three, where the elderlies maintain commentary:

'Now check this,' he says. 'It's twenty after three! In the a.m. already! Where we're going?'

'Twenty after three!' she says.

I keep on smiling. He climbs from the seat, steps into the aisle, breathes hard, staggers once, settles, then takes a bag from the over-head, and he sits again, relieved—woo-eeh!—and he breaks out the pill bottles.

'Put on your eye glasses, Alvin,' she says.

I picture the pills at work. I picture them thinning the blood and checking arrhythmia. I picture the pills as janitors of liver and spleen, wearing jaunty work caps and polite grimaces, making min-imum wage. The snow is banked deeply and the ice fields glisten for as far as you can see.

'These the ten o'clocks?' she says.

'These the tens,' he says, 'though now it's like three. Officially. Where we're going.'

'Twenty after!' she says.

'Twenty after,' he says.

'Put on your eye glasses, Alvin,' she says.

'They're right here on my goddamn face, Rose,' he says.

It is the moment of the mudwater coffee, and we set forth along the aisles. We pour it from the stained tall silver pots, and they suck that bad stuff down, and a low drone of talkativeness rises across the rows. We hit turbulence. It gets good and jumpy, it gets good and swoony, and they look to us, with small brave smiles.

The fade of a melon sun glows over the vast country, in birthday card tones, and it is all of it primordial and ancient seeming down there: National Geographic. The clouds thicken and we enter them and it all whites out but in places the clouds are patchy, and we're allowed a quick cold view below, and you cannot but imagine yourself lost down there.

'DVT is what it is, Rose,' he says. 'That's Deep... Vein... Thrombosis. Travelling clots!'

'Clots travel?' she says.

'Clots hit the brain and you're dead before they get you to the ground. It don't matter what age or creed you are. That's DVT is what it is.'

'Clots in the brain! Sounds like that's about it, hon.'

'Clots in the brain is the last thing we need, trust me.'

'Deep... Vein?'

'Thrombosis. But it's dummies that get DVT, Rose. Dummies that drink on planes and don't move around none. That's what you got not to do! Drink and sit there like a sack of shit.'

It is the moment of the wipes. We pick up the trays, with their lurid remains—dig the color of that masala—and we hand out the wipes. We keep on smiling. Transatlantics pull from each demographic, each ethnicity. There are thin English pub girls bronzed from the effluent beaches of the west coast. There are fat Italians, amused Indians, Germans amplifying sternly, irritated Swiss. Put us in a tin can at 28,000 feet and we become so obviously of our breed.

There is a majorly dramatic sound from the internals—*Kerrrrrr-unnnchhhh!*—like gears changing in God's pick-up. We look to each other across the aisles—the questioning arch of our savagely plucked eyebrows—but we keep on smiling. We are about done with wipes. We make it back to our stations. We smile. Then the *kerrrrrr-unnnchhhh* again, but this time deeper sounding, and Mel and Kelvin talk to flight crew.

Flight crew doesn't tell cabin crew shit unless it has to. There are agitated noises from the rows-of-three and the rows-of-six. There is concern in the seal pens. Kelvin is at the handset: Kelvin pales. Mel is at the handset: Mel gets flushes. The captain now addresses the rows-of-three and the rows-of-six.

He says there is no cause for immediate concern. I like that immediate. The problem, he says, is mechanical. As opposed to?

There is an instrument, there is a device, we needn't worry our pretty heads about what it is precisely, but it's out by, like, millimetres? By like fractions of millimetres. It needs to be recalibrated. This needs to be done on the ground. We look out the windows and down to the ice fields.

Our captain is a Brit and as he addresses us all, he retains an admirable calm. He says a landing is required, actually, and this will be achieved shortly. He actually says the 'actually'. He actually says 'achieved'. We keep on smiling. Our captain is out of a black-and-white war movie. He's an okay-chaps-let's-synchronise-our-watches. He's a chin-up-wren-twill-soon-be-over.

Seat belts on, seat backs up, tables clipped. The ice below us is apparently Greenland ice. The passengers remain pretty calm. They are somewhat inured to in-flight dramatics now—they've seen it all a thousand times. Stabiliser hormones seep, rivers of feel-good juices flow, and everybody is real smug about how well they're holding up.

Then, out of nowhere, a heavy-set man with big hair three seats from the top of cheap gets a flash of realism and he screams out. He shouts at us all, he shouts that he always knew death would come for him in this way, and at this time!

It takes just one shitbird to freak out and now the whole plane gets The Fear. Mel and Kelvin launch into action. They forcibly quieten the fat fuck with an injection. We keep trank spikes for this purpose but we don't advertise the fact. Mel and Kelvin work out.

The plane descends, much more sharply than usual. We eat up huge gulps of air. We are light-headed and we keep on smiling. When the captain said a landing, I guess everybody pictured some snowy little airport for Greenlanders. But there is no airport. There is an ice field. Technically, we call this C.D.I.T.—controlled descent into terrain.

He brings the plane down smoothly. It is a perfect manouevre, flawless, there is hardly a bump. The rows-of-three and the rows-of-six all applaud with great vigour, there are whoops and hollers, but the applause fades quickly as we look out the windows. Visibly the windows fog up with freeze, like in timelapse photography. Mel and

Kelvin call a cabin crew huddle.

There has been information from flight crew. We have to get off the plane. We have to use the emergency slides. We have got to keep the people moving. We have got to keep the people warm. First task is we hand out brandy miniatures for calm. We take to the aisles.

'I'm sorry, ma'am, I cannot drink this stuff,' says a corporate. 'I react against spirits. It's, like, a peptic thing?'

'Drink the fucking brandy,' I say.

I keep on smiling.

The rumours start. There are rumours of an engine fire. There is a rumour of potential explosions. There are rumours of Middle Easterns with dart guns. The emergency slides go down. We slide from the plane. This is not so bad, if you aren't Alvin or Rose, if you do not have hips of titanium. We scuttle from the plane and slip across the ice in a fretful, hard-breathing slapstick. The cold is almost comical: you're-kidding-me cold. We shepherd everybody together in the lee of this like… shale outcrop? Like I know a shale outcrop from shit, but the words have come into my head for some reason… shale outcrop.

We are all together on the ice, a true democracy: flight crew, cabin crew, cheap seats, business. We tell them to wear the life jackets for warmth. We hand out smother blankets too. It is almost summer here. The captain makes a brief speech. He says radio contact has been achieved, actually. He says help will be along very very soon.

Then Kelvin makes a speech. This is Kelvin's Big Moment. This is what it has all been leading up to and Kelvin, he glows. Cabin crew, we all regard Kelvin with awe now. Kelvin has demonstrated The Stuff. His tone is light-hearted and downhome. He says, folks, believe it or not, there is official strategy in these situations. He says, you've seen those documentary shows on Discovery Channel about penguins in the Arctic? He says in winter, the penguins form enor-mous concentric circles, they circle together on the ice, they circle endlessly, move their little feet from side to side, like a revolving chorus line. Folks, says Kelvin, this is how the penguins keep warm and alive! And, basically, folks, this is what we got to do now.

We form on the ice into concentric circles. We move about, we rotate, we get the hang of the penguin stuff real easy, in fact, and it works, it keeps us a couple of degree fractions above blue-veined death. We flap our arms. The way the circles work mean you rotate in and out of many conversations. The talk spins slowly around.

'I mean that's a whole heap of tundra, you know what I'm saying? I mean what does real estate go for out here?'

'Yeah we could make like rudimentary ploughs and settle the place.'

'Now you're farmin'!'

'The nearest town I suppose is... what, Upernavik?'

'Party town?'

'And this is summer, right?'

'I would have to say that I'm anti-pastoral, essentially. Clouds, skies, mountains? Piece of shit.'

'It's like, hey, here's another thousand miles of beauty.'

'She's as if she's on some kind of emotional Slimfast.'

'My husband is like one of those second-hand books you buy that's got all the wrong bits underlined.'

'So I say to her, you sayin' you ain't seen him since Tuesday? You say he ain't been around? Blah blah blah. She goes, naw, I ain't seen him, I been down my sister's, I been over my mum's. Blah blah blah.'

'Blah, blah, blah, yeah? X, y, zee.'

'Lying cow.'

'There is a light. There is a bridge. And they're all on the other side of the bridge, beckoning, calling you across.'

'They're the last people I'd want to see.'

'You think the cold could freeze the watches, Alvin?'

'Then they took over the TV station. They played sombre martial music, interrupted by calls for calm.'

'Yes on the boat now six months many islands no alcohol! Just beer. That is how Pacific islands is yes? No alcohol! I am Portugal originally. The arrest was illegal.'

'I feel I've come to a point where I've exhausted the entire form. It can't hold me anymore. I need to move on.'

'She said she wouldn't decide until the cast came off.'

'First they said clear, now they're saying secondary.'

'He is my son, yes! He is flesh and blood! But what can I say? The motherfucker is out of control!'

'Then he wrapped the car around a lamppost outside Shinrone. End of story. The guard said it wasn't quick, it was slow.'

There is no sign of rescue. There is no movement at all on the white horizon. There is no signal in billowing smoke. Now I feel it creep over the tundra, I know that it will quickly be among us and it is. And death, it turns out, is a complete B-movie ham. Death is cold fingers lightly placed on the back of the scalp. Death is cheesy as a ghost train.

'Emily Brontë was always very weak, even as a child. Reading a book, she'd fall into the fireplace.'

'Says, you gonna grow this business? I look asshole in the eye, I say yes sir I am! Says, you don't know diddly about growing no business. I say, you fuck! You shit for brains!'

'Then I had a chipper for a while, this was in Clonmel.'

The light fades and we continue to circle. We put away brandy miniatures, whisky miniatures, gin miniatures. The vodka is about done already. There has been a run on the vodka. Mel is shitfaced. Mel is giving it some to the French hottie with the tiny feet.

'Very cocktaily, very cha-cha-cha? With those outdoor heaters you know what I'm saying? So you can like sit on the sidewalk in winter even. If that is what you want to do.'

'How many more years do you think you're going to entertain me by imitating television comedians, Paul?'

'Apparently it was one of the worst credit ratings ever recorded in the northwest.'

'I'm not even supposed to be on an aeroplane. Fact!'

'How'd you pitch this? Nobody would believe this shit! They'd be, like, get the fuck out of here asshole!'

'So what you're saying is you're one of these high-functioning alcoholics, basically?'

'I know that! Who do you think you're talking to here? I know the phrase "prose poem" has certain connotations. But bear with me, please.'

'I think you're a very attractive woman. For your age. And I don't mean that in a catty way. Age is only time. And what's time? I'm reading a lot of cosmology at the moment. Your idea of time might be completely different to mine, which is going to be completely different again to what the goat farmer in the Andes is thinking. I mean what's a day? What's a year? Who's to say everybody doesn't have a different idea of a minute? But then I think, should we even think about this stuff?'

'It's a condition called ductalsis. It's a morbid compulsion to weep. They're after isolating a gene for it.'

'When I'm making bread, I'm not just kneading dough, 'kay? What I'm doing, I'm puttin' the love in.'

'This is nothing. One time I was flying from Ukraine? You know like Kiev? On this piece of crap Aeroflot plane? And they're saying we got to make a stop in like Belarus? I'm, like, Belarus?'

'When your time is up your time is up.'

'Everything is predestined.'

'Jesus' love never failed me yet.'

Night-time comes and the talk fades. We continue to circle as we eat the crackers and pretzels that are the last of the food and we drink the last of the miniatures. Alvin leaves us. I comfort Rose, or try to at least. She says, don't be sorry, it was a very gentle thing. The sky is enormous with many stars. The aurora borealis shows up and does its thing—superior discothéque—and everybody is wowed. An army of snowmobiles arrives from Upernavik, buzzing over the snow like some kind of giant sleek ice beetles. They are in pastel colours and the atmosphere they make is festive, like an adventure snow weekend. We are all congratulated because two dead (a young Italian man, also) is an amazing result. Everybody is pretty drunk. Alvin and the Italian lie in bodybags on the ice. Rose is making sound use of the bagful of pills. Rose is seeing the lights.

Later, a fresh plane. We cut down past the Scottish isles, we can see the green boxed fields and great swathes of the bleak cities. And then it's rainy London, finally, in its shockingly humdrum morning. There is a sense of hush and terrific pride. We open the doors. We give the signal. We keep on smiling. We say: Thank you! You have a great trip now! Thank you!

Everybody is hungover and newborn. Fear climbs in fearless ascent but always it fades, it breaks up like jet trail in the air. Now everybody is greenlighted. Now everybody is bulletproof.